SHOOTOUT AT SKAGWAY

by

VAL THAME

First Published 2006

Copyright © Valerie Thame

Typesetting and printing arranged by
Leaf Books Writers' Services
www.leafbooks.co.uk

Printed by Jem
Jem.co.uk

ISBN: 1-905599-28-5
ISBN: 978-1-90-55-99-28-8

Author Contact Details

7 Welbeck Close
Farnborough
Hampshire
GU14 0HD

ONE

Dustbowl, Colorado July, 1897

The constant hammering and pounding invaded Jed's semi-comatose brain with shards of intense pain. He tried to dull the noise by pulling the blanket over his head but it offered little respite.

'Cut it out, will you?' cried Jed. 'Cut it out!'

More pain. His throat felt as dry as a donkey's scrotum and the smell of stale piss filled his nostrils. He turned over, reaching for a pillow, but there was none. The bed was hard and his shoulders bruised. The unremitting hammering, he now realised, was inside his own head. Heaving himself up onto his elbow, he looked groggily towards the light, which came from a small barred window way up near the ceiling.

'Okay, mister. Time to go! Get up!'

Jed squinted up at the thin, mean-faced man standing over him. 'Who the hell are you?' he growled.

'I'm the Town marshal. On your feet cowboy! I've got work to do and you ain't part of it.'

Jed sat up, retrieved his hat from the floor and jammed it on his aching head. 'What happened? What am I doing here?'

'You got in a fight and landed up in jail. Come on. On your feet.' Jed was hustled out of the cell and into the outer office. 'Now, this here's what you came in with. Guns two, gunbelt one....' The marshal took Jed's belongings out of the drawer and dumped them unceremoniously on the desk, '...and dollars, ten.'

Jed's head suddenly cleared. 'Ten dollars? Where's my payroll?'

'No payroll. Sign this and....'

'Hey, hold on,' said Jed, 'you ain't telling me I ain't got no payroll. Six months I worked for that money. Six months herding stinking, no-brain cattle. Now, don't you tell me I ain't got no payroll!'

'Well, you ain't,' said the marshal, tersely. 'Now take your stuff and get out of here.'

'Like hell I will! Somebody's got my payroll and I ain't going without it!'

Jed brought his fist down on the desk.

'Look, cowboy, you blew into town yesterday, full of yourself. If you had any money – you must have spent it. All I know is you started a fight and I put you in jail. Now, you've had you fun and its time to move on!'

Jed strapped on his belt and stuffed the ten-dollar bill in his pocket. 'I don't call having my payroll lifted any kind of fun. You sure you ain't seen it?'

The marshal's lean back stiffened. 'I am an officer of the law, mister, and I just hope you ain't saying something you shouldn't!'

'What about my horse?' said Jed. 'That gone too?'

'I wouldn't know. It's most likely where you left it. Now get out of here. I don't want to see you no more.'

Once in the fresh air, Jed's headache returned with a vengeance. He staggered along the sidewalk cursing and swearing until he passed a horse trough. He stopped, plunged his head into the water, splashed his face and beard and combed his hair with his hand. It made him feel a little better but his clothes still stank of jail. He needed some new duds, a bath and a shave but ten dollars was not going to cover it.

He found his horse saddled-up and tethered outside the saloon and walked it back to the trough for a drink. The horse was thirsty which re-minded Jed how long it had been since he too had had a proper drink.

Two whiskies later he was feeling much better.

'Like to buy a girl a drink, mister?'

A curvaceous redhead in a tight-fitting, purple dress leaned back against the bar and smiled up at him. Jed returned her interest with a dazzling smile that shone through his dark, curly beard. 'Reckon I might.'

'Hey Joe!' The redhead called the bartender over. 'Two whiskey's and we'll take them upstairs in my room.'

'Hey,' said Jed, 'you're way ahead of me lady.'

'What's the problem? Ain't I pretty enough for you?'

'Oh sure. Real pretty. It's just that, well, I'm moving on.'

'Why? You only just got here.' She moved even closer, stretching her arm across the bar in front of him. 'My name's Mary-Anne,' she purred, 'What's yours?'

'Jedediah, though I'm mostly called Jed.' He lifted the glass of whiskey to his lips and emptied it. As he placed it back on the counter he gently moved her arm away and stood back a little from the bar. 'Enjoy your drink, Mary-Anne.' He touched the brim of his hat and was about to leave but Mary-Anne, hands on hips, was in his way.

'I ain't finished, Jedediah. You wouldn't leave a girl to drink on her own now would you?'

'Look ma-am,' said Jed, 'I had a bit of bad luck yesterday. Now, I think you're real pretty and there's nothing I'd like better than to buy you another drink and … well, enjoy the pleasure of your company but the fact is, I've been cleaned out. I only got here yesterday and this morning I woke up in jail with a sore head and empty pockets. So, you see, I can't oblige you right now – not in any way.'

'Well, that's right disappointing but I think I might be able to oblige you.'

Jed's appreciative eyes took in her slim hips, her neat little waist and her bright blue eyes and he was right sure she could do exactly that.

'I have Information you might be interested in,' she said.

'Like?' said Jed.

'Like who cleaned you out.'

'Go on.'

'I was there. I saw what happened. A bunco man swung into town yesterday playing the shell game and he soon drew a crowd. You know what folks are like in these small towns. Nothing much happening - except the odd gunfight. So a bunco game gets a lot of attention but these games are all fixed. They let a few suckers win a couple of dollars and then they're hooked. Double your money! It's that easy, they say. I saw you put down five dollars and you won ten.'

'And somebody in the crowd lifted my payroll while I was playing, is that right? You tell me who it was, Mary-Anne, and I'll kill 'em.'

'Easy, mister. It wasn't like that. You were the biggest sucker of all. I couldn't believe my eyes. After winning twenty dollars you put a wad of greenbacks on the table.'

'I did?'

'You sure did. And you are not a good loser, Jedediah.'

'Like hell I'm not. That was my payroll. Are you saying he took me for $600 dollars?'

'Yeah, and you darned near killed him for it. If it hadn't been for folks pulling you off I think you might have done. Trouble was, you were ready to fight anybody who got in your way but, luckily, the Town marshal turned up and you know the rest'

'What happened to the cheatin' Bunco man. Did I get him?'

'Nope. Slippery as an eel that one. While you were fighting and all, he hi-tailed it out of town.'

'With my money.'

'Yep. And other folks too. You ain't alone. How about another drink, Jed? On me this time?'

Several whiskies later, and ten dollars lighter, Jed left the saloon, and the compassionate arms of Mary-Anne, untied his horse and swung into the saddle. He was going to find that cheating Bunco man and get his money back. Mary-Anne had given him a good description. Tall, lean, dressed in a black suit, sallow complexion with a black beard. But better than that she had discovered, Lord knows how - but women like her have their ways, that he was going North towards Seattle. There was news of another gold rush in the Klondike and that's where he was heading.

'Can't thank you enough, Mary-Anne. I'm going after him.'

'Jed.' Mary-Anne's eyes were pleading with him to stay, and they were so tempting. 'Jed. Must you do this? He's a sharp operator and no man's fool. It ain't worth it.'

'It is to me, but I thank you kindly for your concern.'

'Don't mix with him, Jed. I hear tell he's got a reputation.'

'What sort of reputation? A swindler?'

'Yeah, swindler, cheat and ruthless killer.'

Jed looked at her sharply. 'You know this for sure?'

'No, but there ain't no smoke without fire. You take care. Keep well out of his sights.'

Jed promised he would do just that and gave her one last, lingering kiss of goodbye. It was a pity it was goodbye because he fair took to Mary-Anne but she had her business and he had his. The marshal was standing outside his office, smoking a cheroot, as Jed rode out of town.

Jed raised his hat as he passed by. 'Just leavin', marshal. Anything else I can do for you?'

'Yeah! Don't come back!'

Jed treated the lawman to one of his brightest smiles as he replaced his hat. Unimpressed, the marshal spat on the sidewalk and returned to his office.

Jed had not gone more than a couple hundred yards when he was suddenly brought to a halt by two men who came out of nowhere and, grabbed the reins of his horse. The younger man had several cuts and bruises on his face and the older one was squinting through a monstrous black eye. Both looked like they had been in a recent fight.

'Hold on there, mister. Just where d'you think you're goin'?' said the older of the two.

'Ain't none of your business,' said Jed, 'and take your hands off my horse.'

'Not till you've given my boy Billy his money.'

'Yeah! Give Billy his money,' repeated the boy, who was clearly younger in the head than he was grown.

'I don't know what you're talking about,' said Jed.

'Well, let me tell you mister?' said Billy's father. 'You was at that bunco game yesterday - I saw you so don't deny it - and you stole ten dollars off my boy.'

'Now how'd I do that?' said Jed. 'I ain't never seen you before.'

'You took it when you lost your bet. My Billy had put ten dollars on one of those shells. When you lost your temper, that bunco man took off with your money, but he left my Billy's on the table. I saw you take it but I couldn't get to you quick enough. When that fight broke out I caught a punch on the head and went down.'

'What you saw or thought you saw ain't proof of nuthin'. Get out of my way, the both of you.'

Jed pulled on the reins and swung his horse's head round. The boy Billy stepped back but his father would not let go.

'It ain't fair!' he cried, 'The boy don't understand. He's simple, see. You give him his money back.'

'I can't. I ain't got ten dollars. I'm broke.'

Jed thought that would be the end of it but the irate father was determined to wrestle Jed out of the saddle and get satisfaction somehow. In the commotion the horse reared up and the old man was knocked to the ground just inches from the thrashing hooves. Jed expertly turned the horse aside.

'Pa!' screamed Billy, rushing up to his father who lay unmoving on the ground. 'Say you're not dead Pa! I need you, Pa.'

Jed was out of the saddle and coming to the aid of the old man, but when the son saw him he shouted out, 'You've killed my pa! Keep away from me.'

'Now look boy,' said Jed, 'He started it. If I had the money I'd give it to you. But I ain't.'

But by now the boy was all fired up. He started tugging at his father's coat and pulled out a gun.

'Now look here, boy,' Jed began, but the boy was past being reasoned with. With his hands trembling he pointed the gun at Jed and squeezed the trigger but Jed was quicker and more accurate. The bullet exploded in Billy's thigh. The boy dropped his gun and rolled in the dust, moaning and clutching his injured leg.

The sound of gunfire immediately brought the marshal and others out onto the sidewalk but Jed had no mind to stay and explain. He hoped the old man was not dead, and he knew he had only injured the boy, but even, so he reckoned he had well and truly outstayed his welcome in Dustbowl.

Jed lit out of town like a steer in a stampede. Behind him he could hear shouts of 'Sonofabitch!' and 'String him up!' but that didn't signify. Anybody who wanted to do that would have to catch him first.

TWO

It was only an hour or so after sundown when Jed rode into Barker's Creek. It looked a sleepy little place but not so sleepy they would serve him a second whiskey in the Silver Dollar Saloon without seeing the colour of his money. His vigorous protests only led him to being thrown out.

A soft voice in the darkness said, 'Want to do business, mister?'

He turned, his hand automatically covering his holster, to see one of the women from the saloon sitting on the sidewalk. Her feet were in the road and her skirt hitched up well above her knees showing her red petticoats. She was not young, nor any kind of beauty but the evening shadows, and the single whiskey on an empty stomach, had the desired effect on Jed.

'Why?' he said, 'You got any ideas what a man might do at this time of night?'

He sat down beside her and at the same time eased her low-cut dress a little further off her shoulders so that he could kiss the swell of her breasts. She looked up at him, eyes shut and lips slightly parted. It was an invitation Jed could not resist. He leaned forward.

'You smell sweet, mister,' she said, suddenly tipping her chin. 'You got money?'

'Sure,' lied Jed, his arm around her waist. 'Plenty! But will you be worth it?'

The woman laughed. It was a deep, coarse laugh. 'Belle ain't never disappointed nobody! Ask around.'

She stood up but Jed remained seated, his hand reaching up her legs to her soft thighs. She stopped his hand travelling further and whispered, 'I have a private room upstairs, mister.'

Half an hour later he was being pushed out of an upstairs window, and an enraged Belle was screaming, 'And you can take these with you, an' all! You cheating liar. I should've got you to pay first!'

Jed fell heavily onto the roof of the sidewalk and rolled into the street quickly followed by his pants and boots. As he pulled on his clothes Belle continued to scream obscenities at him from the saloon window including derogatory remarks about his sexual prowess. These were quickly taken up, and elaborated on, by a group of men tumbling out of the saloon.

'Yeah? You weren't so hot either!' he shouted back at Belle. 'But not bad for nuthin'.'

'Nuthin? I got your gunbelt, ain't I?'

The window slammed down. The young men whooped and whistled and a couple of old-timers sitting outside the saloon called out to Jed as he stuffed his feet into his boots. He felt so naked and vulnerable without his gunbelt. He had to get that back. No woman was worth that kind of sacrifice.

'She don't do no favours, our Belle,' said one of the old timers.

'Yeah?' said Jed. 'Well, she sure didn't do me none!'

He still had griping hunger pains in his stomach but his first need was to find somewhere to bed down. He walked the roan to the edge of town and tied it to a tree. Then he calmly rolled under the sidewalk. As good a place as any for the night.

The following morning, after a sluice in the horse trough, Jed gave some thought to food and finding work knowing both would be difficult. Barker's Creek was small and the shopkeeper's kept a wary eye out for strangers, like Jed, who might be up to no good. After trying, unsuccessfully, to help himself he found a few coins in his pocket, which bought him a small pie and a beer.

He had decided that if he found work here he'd put his venture on hold for a while, just long enough to become solvent again. He did not hold out much hope of finding work here and, so far, had not only drawn a blank but raised suspicions among the townsfolk. His last call was at the Dustbowl Livery Stables which was run by a blacksmith called Joe Peterson.

'Where you from?' asked Joe, a thin, wiry old man, who was vigorously pumping the bellows at the fire. He was well past his best but still as strong as an ox. 'Ain't see you before!'

'No, that's right,' said Jed. 'I've been drifting for a while. Since my ma and pa died, I was the only child, see. Couldn't run the farm on my own. Just a kid, you know?' Jed had told this story so many times he was beginning to believe it himself. 'Ain't got no trade in particular but I'm willing and strong. '

'OK. I can give you work,' said Joe, 'but you don't get paid till the end of the day and if you don't do a good job, then you don't get no pay.'

'That's straight enough,' said Jed.

'Any chance of some breakfast before I start?' Jed was still very hungry.

Joe Peterson frowned. 'It'll come off your wages.'

'That's fine,' said Jed. Joe offered him a welcome piece of apple pie and a chunk of bread. 'How about lodgings, Mr Peterson? You know any good lodgings round here?'

'I might do.' The old man looked him up and down. 'You clean and tidy in your habits?'

'I surely am,' said Jed.

'D'you you read the bible?'

'Every day,' said Jed, a lie, which bought him a bed in the Peterson household.

At the end of a long, hard day attending to fractious, unco-operative horses and pumping the forge bellows, Jed felt he had more than earned his pay. That evening Mrs Peterson, a plump, homely woman in a check apron, her once-fair hair tied round her head in neat plaits, welcomed Jed to her home. She showed him to a sparkling clean but plainly furnished, white painted room in the loft space, accessed by a simple wooden ladder. She also brought him some hot water and towels, which she set down at the bottom of the ladder.

'For a shave I am thinking,' she said, twiddling an imaginary beard on her smooth, plump chin. 'Supper vill be ready soon.'

Jed thanked her kindly but a shave was the last thing on his mind. He might look as though he needed one because his beard was wild and curly but that's the way it was and he had gotten used to it being there. Anyhow, he thought, once you started shaving there was no end to it.

His shirt smelled of the labours of the day; coal dust, horses and sweat so he took it off and hung it out of the window to air. He did not smell too fragrant and certainly needed a wash. To please Mrs Peterson, he thought he might trim his beard – just a little. As he tidied himself up he tried to think of ways of making more money. He didn't reckon working at the forge Joe would make his fortune. Joe was a hard taskmaster. Jed had spent a long hot day sweating his guts out and for what? A few measly dollars. At this rate he'd be stuck in Dustbowl for the next five years before he could make enough money to get to Seattle, and no hope at all of getting to the Klondike.

As he was making the final adjustments to his beard he thought of his lost payroll and how easily it had been lifted in that shell game.

'I can't be the only gambling fool that ever lived. There must be other suckers like me just waiting to be fleeced.' The thought made him smile. 'And if others can do it and get away with it, so can I.'

Feeling a deal more cheerful he climbed down the ladder into the main room where something, which smelled real tasty, was bubbling on the stove.

'Bean stew,' said Mrs Peterson. 'A favourite of my boys. Mr Peterson and I had four,' she told him proudly, 'and all vis goot appetite. Sit yourself down and eat.'

She ladled a generous helping of stew into Jed's bowl and cut off a hunk of bread from a freshly baked and sweet smelling loaf. This was Jed's first decent meal since he'd left the Lucky K Ranch with his fine fat payroll, although his head told him it was only a few days ago, his stomach was sure it was much, much longer. He ate hungrily wiping up every last trace of gravy with the crusty bread and all had gone before Mr Peterson started eating.

'It is looking like you could eat more,' said Mrs Peterson, refilling his bowl.

Jed nodded, gratefully. When he had finished the second helping he sat back in his chair and belched with vigour and satisfaction.

'Beg pardon ma-am, but that was a mighty fine stew. Mighty fine. Just like my old ma used to make.'

It was the right thing to say. Thinking of her own boys making their lonely way in the world, homely Mrs Peterson wiped a tear from her eye and patted Jed's shoulder.

'Anything you vant, son. You only got to ask.'

'Well, there is something, ma-am.'

'Eva!' It was a warning from the old man as he got up from the table. 'Don't make no fancy promises you can't keep. He ain't one of our boys. I'll be out on the porch if you need me.'

'All right Joe.' And when he had gone outside. 'Vat is it you are wanting, Jed? Hmmm?'

'Well, I was wondering if'n you had any walnuts, ma-am.'

'Is that all? You like walnut. No problem.' Eva Peterson took a stone jar from her store cupboard and offered the contents to Jed. 'Here, take as many as you want.'

Jed took a slack handful and put them in his pocket. 'This'll do just fine, ma-am, thank you. Reckon I'll go for a stroll now, walk off that fine meal.'

He left the pretty, white-painted house with Joe sitting on the porch smoking his pipe and his wife singing as she washed up the pans. They seemed very happy together, and Jed wondered if the day would ever come when he would be that content or if he would ever find someone with whom to share such contentment. But they were thoughts for the future. Right now he must concentrate on making a few bucks and fast. He walked down to the edge of Barker's Creek. It was cool and quiet under the trees. A good place to think. Before he left he picked up a handful of small stones and pocketed them.

The following night, after another days work and a large Peterson supper inside him, Jed went down to the saloon for a beer. Inside *The Silver Dollar*, Belle was doing her stuff on the stage much to the admiration of the customers. She must have seen Jed come in because, as soon as she had finished her number, she came over to him. She stood beside him, leaning backwards, her elbows on the bar, her ample bosom thrust forward. She looked even less attractive and even older in the harsh light.

'So, you snake-in-the-grass, what makes you think you can take Belle for nuthin' and get away with it.'

She had a couple of mean-looking hard men with her as back up.

'Never thought that for one minute, ' said Jed, smiling broadly. He had white, even teeth and when he smiled he knew he was irresistible to all women - young or old. 'Me, I'm a peaceful kind of guy that was just down on his luck. Things are different now.'

He slapped a few dollar bills on the bar. Belle gave the money a casual glance and then said, 'You think I'm that cheap?'

'You got my gun belt, ain't you?' The two men moved closer and Jed added some more greenbacks. 'That should make us quits,' he said, 'assuming I get my gun belt back.' Belle reached out to take the money but Jed's hand quickly covered hers. Their faces were close. Her eyes were narrowed, her mouth taut and mean. 'But for that kind of money, I'd need to sample the goods again just so's I know I'm getting good value.'

'The pleasure,' said Belle, acidly, 'will be all yours.' She nodded to the two men who turned aside to let them pass. 'Follow me, cowboy.'

She sashayed between the close-packed tables, her dress rippling over the customer's knees, clearly enjoying the attentions of the drunks who clawed at her as she passed. A soiled dove, she ain't, thought Jed as he followed her up the stairs. There was nothing innocent about Belle and nothing dove-like. She didn't know it yet but as soon as he'd got his gunbelt he was going to be out of there.

CHAPTER THREE

L ater, back at the Peterson homestead, with his gun belt back where it belonged, Jed spent what was left of the night practising the shell game. But it would not work. The gravel was way too heavy to manipulate.

In the morning, after one of Mrs Peterson's sizeable breakfasts of bacon and grits, Jed asked if she could let him have some dried peas.

'Not for eating,' she said. 'No. A good soaking they vill need.'

'No, not for eating,' said Jed. 'I couldn't eat another thing.' He patted his stomach.

'So vat for are they?'

'I sort of needs them for an experiment.'

'An experiment? My, my. An experiment.'

Though puzzled Mrs Peterson gave Jed a dish of dried peas and he thanked her kindly, complimenting her on her well stocked store cupboard. The old woman was completely won over. In her eyes, he was a fine young man who could do no wrong. Much like her own dear boys.

That night, after a hearty supper and back in his room, Jed set out the walnut shells and the dried peas on his washstand. He practised *Find the Lady*' every night for the next week. To begin with, he just could not reckon it. The odds should have been in his favour but they were not. He had been trying so hard to make it work that come the Friday his head was all mussed up. He was about to give up when he remembered what the Bunco man in Dustbowl had said - *The swiftness of the hand deceives the eye* - and then it all became clear.

'The darned pea was never under the shell. Sure, it looked like it but I reckon it was slipped under *after* the punter had put his money down.'

So, Jed practised some more, his smile lighting up his face at the thought of the profit to come. He hoped to stay in Barker's Creek for at least another week to perfect his technique but on Saturday old Joe paid him off.

'I ain't got no more work for you and unless you can pay for your board and lodgings you'd best look elsewhere.'

So it was farewell to the Petersons and back on the trail. He left Barker's Creek with twenty-five dollars, the walnut shells and some bread, cheese and water from kindly Mrs Peterson. He'd had a mind to acquire a better saddle from old man Peterson, or at the very least to help himself to a few dollars from his savings, which he had discovered were stored in a tin under old Joe's bed. But his conscience pricked. The elderly couple had been good to him when he most needed help and he just couldn't bring himself to do it.

Several miles on and at the first decent sized town he came to Jed bought himself a fancy suit and a new shirt. Then he straightway rode on to the next, which happened to be a little place called Paradise. It was time to make some money so he set up his Bunco stall on a barrel, outside the only saloon in town - *The Red Garter.* He smiled at passers by and, looking every inch a gentleman, the townsfolk were drawn like bees to a honey pot.

His patter and his confident smile were a winning combination. Within half-an-hour he had made enough money to buy a meal, a bed and a woman but not in Paradise. He had to move on pretty quick. He worked the next two towns on the trail with great success but at the fourth things turned unexpectedly sour. He had done well enough with the shell game to pack up and move on within the hour, but Madame Greed using all her persuasive charms, had whispered in his ear. *'You can see this lot are suckers. There's time for one more game.'*

A young man, his jacket ominously tucked behind two six-shooters, swaggered up to Jed's stall.

'I've got forty dollars in my hand, mister, and I mean to go away with eighty! I consider myself real lucky today. You hear what I say?'

Jed considered the situation. This young buck was threatening him. He was saying - *Let me win or my guns will do the talking.* He was staking a hell of a lot of money and, in spite of the prominent firearms, it was a challenge Jed could not resist.

'Lady Luck is a most capricious companion,' he said as he skilfully moved the shells around the table. 'What is your name, sir?'

'Bryant.'

'Then let's hope she's with you, today, Mr Bryant. Place your bet and good luck!'

The crowd pressed forward sensing the tension between the two men.

'I say the little lady's right there!' said Bryant, putting his forty dollars in front of the middle shell.'

' Want to change your mind?' asked Jed. He always gave the punters this chance. It sounded good and fair but it didn't make any difference to the outcome.

'No, sir. That's where she is. Turn it over.'

The crowd was silent as Jed lifted the shell. It was empty. He quickly scooped up the forty dollars. 'Not so lucky today,' he said, 'and that's the end of the show, folks!'

The man Bryant did not move. 'I don't think you were listening to what I was saying, mister. I was certain sure I was going to be lucky. Lift up those other two shells.'

Jed raised the shells at the same time he dextrously slipped the pea under the right hand one. The thwarted punter stared at the table in dis-belief.

'I don't know how you did it, mister, but the lady was not under that shell.'

'Are you accusing me of cheatin'?' Jed was anxious to get away and his patience was wearing thin. 'I said that's it for today. Game's over! You lost.' He started to walk away but, by the gasps and reactions of the crowd behind him, he knew something was up and his gun was in his hand as he turned round. Bryant stood alone in the middle of the street, his arm raised and his gun in his hand. Jed heard the unnerving whistle of the bullet as it passed close to his ear but had the satisfaction of know-ing he was unhurt as his opponent fell to the ground, a spreading purple stain on his shirt.

FOUR

Jed left that town with an easy conscience about the killing. It was self-defence. That man Bryant was looking for trouble from the outset, but he also knew that few would be brave enough, or care enough, to stand witness for him. He rode on and on until his horse was too tired to go any further and he stopped overnight in a run-down shantytown miles from anywhere.

Then it was back on the road to fleece the gullible and fatten his wallet as well as to spend his money in the saloons on liquor and women. It was an easy life and he was enjoying it even though he left every town he visited with cries of 'fraudster' and 'swindler' ringing in his ears. But he paid no mind to it. Sometimes, of course, the crowds got ugly and Jed had no option but to defend himself in the only way he knew. In the larger towns, the local lawman would be summoned but Jed never hung around long enough to make his acquaintance.

Jed's reputation travelled fast and he was now a wanted man in several places. But the law in one state did not necessarily apply in the next and Jed used this to his advantage. Not that he ever saw himself as a bad man or a murderer. He only ever killed in self-defence – never in cold blood.

Over the coming months he drifted north, hopefully following in the footsteps of the man who had originally cheated him in the bunco game. In Jed's eyes this was a wrong that had to be made good. The fact that he had been lining his own pockets by robbing folks blind, and using exactly the same technique, did not affect his need for revenge.

After spending a while in Salt Lake City, he went on into Wyoming, then to Idaho and by the time he got to Oregon, he had replaced his six-month's pay three times over - and spent it too. It was in Oregon that he saw a wanted poster pinned to a fence that gave him a nasty shock. Staring back at him was his own face. Dark hair and bushy beard, and above the picture the words 'Wanted for Murder.' On closer inspection he could see the poster referred to a man called Soapy Smith who was a cheat, swindler and murderer. Angrily, Jed tore the poster down. He could easily be mistaken for this no-good rogue. He studied the poster again. The face was familiar for another reason too. It was the same man who had lifted his payroll back in Dustbowl. Jed fingered his growth of unruly beard thoughtfully. He would miss it after all this time but something told him now was the time to shave it off and the sooner the better. He folded the poster, carefully, and put it in his pocket.

Profitable though it had been, Jed had tired of the shell game and needed to do something else. Something different. But what? It was a new day and a new town but he did not feel like working a crowd. Instead, he moseyed into the local saloon, *The Golden Garter*. There were not many customers inside, just a few old timers and one or two others, but as he leaned on the bar, waiting to be served, a stranger got up from one of the tables and stood beside him. Knowing he had never set foot in this town before in his life, Jed was instantly alert.

'Bar ain't busy, mister,' said Jed, without looking up. 'Plenty of room up the other end.'

'Jed Hansen, ain't it?' said the man. 'I've heard about you.'

Jed's hand hovered over his holster. 'Oh yeah? And what have you heard?'

'I've heard you're a fast talker and have made a deal of money out of a Bunco game.'

Jed's fingers curled round the handle of his Colt .45. 'So? You a law man?'

The stranger smiled. 'No, indeed sir!'

Jed took a good, long look at the man beside him. He was average height, not tall, neatly dressed in a brown suit and in his early forties, maybe. Not the sort you normally found in a saloon unless they were looking for something other than alcohol.

'Why are you so interested in me,' he said, 'and how d'you know my name?'

'Your name and reputation go before you, Mr Hansen. Allow me to introduce myself. My name's Penfold. William B. Penfold.' The man held out his hand but Jed ignored it. Seemingly unconcerned Penfold continued. 'I'm in a similar line of business to yourself and I have a proposition I'd like to put to you. Can I buy you a drink?'

Jed's curiosity was aroused. 'Sure.'

'A bottle of your best bourbon, bartender, and two glasses, if you please. And we'll be over there.' Penfold waved towards a table under the stairs.

'You see, Mr Hansen,' said Penfold, once they were seated, 'I know a sure-fire way of making money but it needs someone like you and a hell of a lot of soap.'

'Soap?' queried Jed. 'Is this some kind of joke, mister? Are you insinuating I smell? That I need a wash?'

'Certainly not, sir,' said Penfold. 'The soap is just part of it. But it's an absolutely vital part.' The drinks arrived and Penfold poured two shots, raised his glass to Jed, and downed the contents. 'Aaah! That's better. You see, I need somebody who can pull a crowd, who can charm the birds out of the trees, somebody who can look after himself and somebody who has money.'

'No need to go no further, Mr Penfold. I see the way your mind is going. You want my money. Well, I ain't wet behind the ears,' Jed finished his drink and stood up. 'You'd best look elsewhere.'

'Don't be too hasty, Mr Hansen. May I call you Jed? Sit down, Jed. Sit down. Money is only a small part of my plan. Why you have so many attributes, it seems to me you fit the bill right well. Believe me,' he lowered his voice,' there's profit in this venture. Big profit. Another drink?' He filled Jed's glass.

'How did you know I was here?' said Jed. 'Didn't know I'd be here myself 'til I arrived!'

'I had the pleasure of watching you operate in Paradise. Slick, real slick and I thought, straightaway, that's the man I need. I've been trailing you ever since.'

'So what's the deal?'

'Well, I got the idea of this little money-spinner from a man called Smith. You heard of him?'

'Yeah,' said Jed. 'Who ain't? I heard he'd sell his own mother for a dollar. Don't he operate up Skagway, somewheres.'

'Indeed he does, and I hear he's a very rich man.'

'So why ain't you rich?'

Penfold scratched his head. 'I like to think of myself as an *honest swindler*. By that I mean I don't deal with gangsters and the like. Smith? Well, he has different values to me. That is, he don't have any, but I'm not here to talk about him. Now, this idea of mine - all it needs is a little investment. You see, I need to purchase a considerable quantity of soap.'

'Ah!' grunted Jed. 'Now why ain't I surprised. Well, my money's hard-earned, mister, and I ain't fixing to give it to no stranger to buy soap.'

'Trust me,' said Penfold, tipping the bottle yet again. 'Put your trust and your money in my business, and you'll double it, treble it.'

'Why, that's just the sort of line I just might use myself,' said Jed. He was understandably suspicious but at the same time intrigued by William B. Penfold and his proposition.

'Well, it's like this,' said Penfold, leaning conspiratorially across the table. 'We need a horse and wagon and as much soap as we can buy. We drive out to a place that hasn't seen either of us before and you start selling the soap.'

'Look. I ain't no soap salesman, mister.'

'Hold on there. Hear me out will you? Some of the bars of soap will have dollar bills concealed inside the wrappers. Some of them $10 dollar bills a $20 dollar bill and maybe a $50 dollar bill.'

'A $50 dollar bill?' Jed poured himself another drink. 'How in hell's name are you ever gonna make a profit if you're giving away $50 dollar bills?'

'That's why it has to be two of us. While you're selling the soap I'm in the crowd, see. Now what Soapy did was clever, real clever. He made a big show of wrapping the bars in front of the punters. He waved a $20 bill in the air so's everybody could see it, then by sleight of hand, I say, sleight of hand the money went into his pocket. It didn't go in the bar at all. What d'you think of that? Poor fools couldn't wait to buy the soap and he made a fortune.'

'I see. But how'm I gonna do that? I ain't no magician.'

'No. You don't have to be, see! You just need to look good and be convincing. And you do. I've seen you operate.'

'So how do we get round the giving away money problem? Don't rightly see it yet?'

'Well, that's where my special plan comes in. We, you and me, wrap the soap beforehand. The bar with the $50 bill, or any others, is specially marked. You sell me the marked bar. I unwrap it and make a big show of finding the money. That'll start other folks buying.'

Jed considered this. 'What about when nobody else gets lucky? Could be nasty.'

'Well, we'll take a chance on losing a couple of tens here and there, just to keep the crowd happy. But I tell you, Jed, they'll buy anything for the chance of winning fifty dollars! Heck, I might even slip in a $100 bill, and at five dollars for a two-bit bar of soap we're gonna clean up anyway. Ha! Pardon my joke. If Soapy Smith can do it so can we just so long as we don't hit the same towns that he did.'

Jed's even-toothed grin grew wider as the idea took hold in his mind. He considered its possibilities while Penfold fidgeted impatiently in his chair.

'So? What do you say? '

'Well, I ain't averse to a bit of honest swindling.'

Good. And we split the takings 50-50? OK?'

'60-40,' said Jed. 'In my favour. After all, I'm the one in the firing line and it's my money we're gonna use to buy the soap! '

'Done!' said Penfold.

They shook hands on the deal and finished the bottle. Then, after making arrangements to meet the following day, Penfold left. Jed sat for a while rehearsing in his mind exactly what he had to do when a sweet voice whispered in his ear, 'You got anywhere to sleep tonight, mister?'

Startled out of his reverie Jed looked up into the smiling face of Mary-Anne.

'Mary-Anne? What are you doing out here?'

'Same as you I reckon. Earning a living. You get tired of the same old bars, same old customers.....if you know what I mean. You found that cheating bunco man yet?'

Jed smiled. 'Nope. Been playing my own game. Not done to badly by it neither.'

'Oh yes. I've heard all about you. Ain't a town from here back to Colorado that don't have your wanted picture pinned up.'

'Picture?' Jed thought of Smith's poster in his pocket. 'You're sure it's me? I mean, lots of people look like me.'

'Well, it ain't so much a picture as a drawing, and it ain't very good because I told that itty-bitty old lawman in Denver that you was bald and cross-eyed!'

Jed laughed. 'You're something else, Mary-Anne. I like your style.'

'Good. I have a room here if you're interested.'

Jed caught her round the waist and pulled her onto his lap. 'That's the best offer I've had for some time,' he said, kissing her soft, smooth neck. 'How much is it gonna cost me this time?'

'Now that depends.'

Mary-Anne was as tasty as she had ever been and Jed made the most of her willing body and wild lovemaking. Whatever it was going to cost him it was worth it. When his passion was spent he lay back on the soft pillows and Mary-Anne cuddled up to him. 'You a bible man?' she said.

'Whatever gave you that idea?'

'The name. Jedediah. Sounds kinda biblical.'

'Well, ma folks were inclined that way. They were Methodists and named me after Jedediah Smith. He didn't drink, didn't smoke, washed every day and didn't take no women. I guess they hoped I'd grow up like my namesake.'

Mary-Anne laughed. I'm mighty glad you didn't. That'd be a real waste of manpower.'

'Yep. I never did quite fit in. Me and my two older brothers were raised on a strong work ethic but I didn't take too kindly to it. I saw my father work himself into an early grave on that dirt patch they called a farm and my mother followed soon after for the same reason. I was fourteen. My brothers took over the farm and expected me to work it like Ma and Pa did, but I wasn't gonna do that. So, I took what money I could find and one of the horses and ran away. Been driftin' ever since.'

They lay quiet after this each with their own thoughts and then Mary-Anne said, 'I couldn't help overhearing your conversation with that man Penfold.'

'That ain't none of your business,' said Jed.

'I'm thinking it could be,' said Mary-Anne, running her expert fingers over his suddenly tense body. 'Seems to me you could do with a woman on a venture like that. I could be somebody in the crowd as well as Penfold. They wouldn't suspect a woman.'

Jed turned to look at Mary-Anne's lovely face. It looked so young and innocent yet Jed knew it hid a cunning brain. 'And you expect us to split the profits three ways. I don't think Penfold would go for that.'

'Ten percent ain't that much and you'd have somebody to keep you warm in bed at nights.'

'I ain't looking to settle down, Mary-Anne, if that's what you're thinking.'

'Jesus! Nor me,' said Mary-Anne. 'I got plans. But I'm heading North. You're heading North. So what do you say?'

Jed considered the offer. 'That's OK. But purely business mind.'

Mary-Anne sat up and offered her hand. 'So it's a deal, then.'

Jed shook it solemnly and then found a more stimulating use for it.

'It's a deal,' he said.

FIVE

The next day both Jed and Mary-Anne were up early. He went down to the livery stables and Mary-Anne to the stores to buy as much soap and brown paper as she could lay her hands on.

The three of them went back to Will Penfold's hotel room and, under his direction, set about wrapping the soap in squares of brown paper to make it look more expensive. Jed and Mary-Anne were in high spirits; joking and laughing but Will was not responding to either of them and seemed mighty put out about something.

'What's wrong, Will?' asked Jed 'You OK?'

'Sure. Say, Mary-Anne, get us some beers from the bar would you, honey? This is thirsty work.'

As soon as Mary-Anne had left the room, Will turned to Jed and said, 'What the hell did you bring her along for? You can get a woman in any saloon. Why'd you have to bring that whore along? I say get rid of her.'

'Well, I ain't getting rid of her and that's that. And you needn't worry about your profit. Her cut is coming out of my share.'

At that Will looked slightly less aggrieved. 'But she'll slow us down. We might need to hole-up sometimes. Live rough. A woman has certain priorities. You know what I mean?'

Jed could see Will had gotten himself worked up. 'If'n it bothered you so much you should have said right at the outset.'

'You didn't give me a chance. '

'No, maybe I didn't. But just you let me deal with it. I think she'll be an asset.'

'Yeah? For who?'

'Give it a rest, Will.'

At that point the door opened and Mary-Anne came in with the drinks. Jed wondered how much she had heard of their conversation but Mary-Anne gave no sign. She put the tray of beers down on the table and sat on the bed cutting the brown paper into neat little squares. As she snipped her thoughtful eyes strayed from Jed, who kept his head down, to Will whose expression was one which surprised her. His eyes ranged over her body with a look that was only too familiar – that of pure lust.

An hour passed and Jed decided to load some of the soap onto the wagon. As soon as he had left the room Will grabbed Mary-Anne by the arms and kissed her roughly on the mouth. She struggled fiercely and when he refused to release her she brought her knee up into his groin. Will fell back gasping and as he did so she slapped his face for good measure.

'I thought you were more of a gentleman!' she raged. 'But I see you ain't. What the hell was that about?'

Will Penfold, having got the worst of that encounter, sat down on the bed breathing heavily.

'Why should he have all the fun?' he nodded towards the door. 'What's one more to women like you?'

For that he received another stinging blow across the face.

'You keep outta my face, Will Penfold, and we'll get along just fine.'

At that moment the door opened and Jed returned.

'Would you believe it,' said Mary-Anne. 'Will here tripped over and fell and hit his head badly on the bed rail. Needs bathing.'

While Jed was pouring some water out of the jug Mary-Anne said, 'Now you mind what I said, Will. You don't want to get hurt again do you?'

By the end of the afternoon all the soap, save three bars, was neatly wrapped and stowed in the wagon. Two $10 bills were tucked inside two wrappers and the $50 dollar bill concealed in the third and Jed had made a small mark on each wrapper so that he'd recognise them again.

Mary-Anne and Jed returned to the saloon the following morning.

'What the hell is that?' spluttered Jed when he saw a large trunk on the backboard of the wagon.

'Well, a girl needs a wardrobe,' said Mary-Anne, climbing up into the driving seat. 'I ain't fixing to look like this for too long.'

Mary-Anne looked every inch a respectable young matron. She wore a plain woollen dress with a shawl and bonnet and carried a small basket on her arm. Jed smiled. No matter what she wore Mary-Anne was going to look darned tasty.

'OK,' said Will, 'Let's get this stuff loaded and get out of here. You hitch your horse to the wagon, Jed, and I'll ride alongside. OK? We're heading for Flint; it's a small settlement a few miles along the trail. When we get within spitting distance I'll go on ahead. You follow when you're good and ready and wait for me on the edge of town. OK?'

Jed nodded. 'OK.'

Flint was just a collection of ramshackle buildings that had very few visitors and even less soap and Will Penfold had already checked it out as likely territory. A mile or so before they got there, Jed stopped and Will rode on ahead as agreed. They had not spoken to each other for the entire journey and it was obvious to Mary-Anne that Jed and Will had had words and she had little doubt that she was the cause.

Jed drove on for another half mile or so then Mary-Anne walked the last few hundred yards into town. Jed still had a while to wait so he took the opportunity to put his feet up and enjoy a cheroot before he made his appearance in Flint. By the time he arrived it was mid afternoon. He drove slowly down the main street stopping at the far end. As was customary with anything new in Flint, Jed soon attracted a fair amount of interest among the settlers.

'What you got in there, mister?' said one old timer.

'Why, sir,' said Jed, all smiles and charm, 'that's for me to know and for you to find out.'

'You selling, mister?' said a woman with a baby. 'Let's see what you've got.'

A few miners came staggering out of the saloon their curiosity aroused. Some children came by and tried to look under the cover.

'It's little parcels,' yelled one.

'What's in 'em?' cried the old timer. 'Why won't you tell us what you got? Are you selling or not?'

'Well now, that's very possible,' said Jed, who had just spotted Will at the back of the crowd 'I was merely passing through but I think you may be interested in what I have.' Neat and dandy in his new black suit and shiny waistcoat he was in stark contrast to the poorly dressed miners and their families who gathered round. He stood up in front of the driver's seat and raised his hat. 'Gentlemen - and ladies. Gather round. I have with me some prime goods which have recently and fortuitously, come into my possession and of which I have an abundance.'

'Speak English!' somebody yelled.

Jed held up a wrapped bar of soap which produced murmurs of interest.

'This, my friends, is soap of the finest quality,' said Jed. Loud groans. 'But not just ordinary soap,' Jed continued. 'Oh no. One of these bars of soap could make you rich.'

A collective and derisive snort came from the crowd.

'How come?' came a voice from the back.

'I will tell you,' said Jed, now well into his showman's patter. 'Hidden in some packets there are ten dollar bills and in others....' he paused dramatically, '...fifty dollars. Buy a bar of my soap and you'll have the chance of making some extra money. At the very least you'll have a mighty fine bar of soap.'

'What's in it for you, mister?' said the old timer. 'Nobody goes giving money away for nothing.'

'I, sir,' said Jed, 'will be selling my excess stock. That is all there is to it. Come along now. Only five dollars a bar. And remember what they say. Cleanliness is next to Godliness.'

The settlers were hesitant. Five dollars for a bar of soap that normally cost a few cents? But the lure of something for nothing, coupled with Jed's smooth talking approach soon won them over. Hands went up, children were sent home for money and five-dollar bills were waved in the air. There was a buzz of excitement as the soap was feverishly unwrapped and then a man in the crowd waved a fifty-dollar bill in the air.

'I got one!' he cried. 'I got fifty dollars. Look.'

'Me too,' cried a woman's voice. 'I got twenty!'

After that the rush was on and Jed could hardly sell them quickly enough, even at five dollars a time. After a while an old miner scooped ten dollars but when nobody else found a greenback the settlers began to smell a rat.

Quick to sense the mood of the crowd Jed whipped up the horse and was out of Flint and out of sight before the dust had settled behind him.

A couple of miles on he stopped to catch his breath and it wasn't long before Will, with Mary-Anne behind, joined him. She slid expertly from the horse's rump into the wagon and up into the driving seat beside Jed. Glowing with excitement she grabbed the reins from Jed.

'Yah!' she yelled. 'Git! You doggone nag. Git!'

The poor wagon horse responded as best it could and they drove on into the night. When she considered she was safe Mary-Anne slowed down.

'Easy money, eh?' said Will, who very soon came alongside. 'Didn't I tell you?'

'You did,' said Jed. 'Where to now?'

'The next town and the next saloon! Yahoo!'

Will clearly had the smell of money in his nostrils and was as excited as Jed had ever seen him.

'No. I say we bed down somewhere quiet for the night,' said Jed. Let things settle a little. We can go looking for excitement tomorrow.'

After a brief protest, and mutterings about finding a woman, Will Pen-fold reluctantly agreed. They rode into a valley and kept going until the trees grew thicker and the sky darker. It was Mary-Anne who first spotted the cabin down by the river. She drew on the reins. The horse snorted and stopped, glad of a rest.

'Looks empty to me,' she said. 'Ain't no smoke.'

'Listen' said Jed.

'Can't hear nothing,' said Will.

'Good,' said Jed. 'That's how I like it. Nonetheless, you stay here with Mary-Anne while I go take a look around.'

The darkness was all enveloping, just the palest of grey light filtering through the trees but enough for Jed to see his way to the cabin his eyes and ears alert for any movement or sound. There was something about the set up that didn't seem right. The cabin was in fairly good condition so where was the occupier? Something else bothered him, the door of the cabin was open and on the porch was a curious bundle of, what appeared to be, old clothes. Once close up Jed could see it was a body. An old man with two gun shot wounds in his chest. Jed surmised this had happened within the last few hours for rigor mortis had not yet set in. The old man was clutching a tin box that had probably contained his life's savings but was empty now.

Cautiously, he stepped over the body and looked inside. It was a one-room cabin with a dirt floor, a stove on one wall and a small box-bed in the corner. There was also wooden cupboard, a table and two chairs. On the table was a tin mug, a plate with some left over remains of a meal and a half-eaten crust of bread. The old man had obviously been taken by surprise by his unexpected visitors and had put up a fight. Jed stood for a few seconds in the doorway and scanned the trees. All seemed as it should be and he hoped that whoever had killed the old man was long gone. He dragged the body round to the back of the cabin, laid him in the undergrowth and kicked some dirt and twigs over him.

'Sorry old timer,' he said, 'Don't mean no disrespect but I can't leave you here in full view. I'll give you a decent burial as soon as I can.'

'Cabin's OK,' he said, when he got back, 'don't look like nobody lives there anymore. It'll do us for tonight.'

'I should just hope so,' said Mary-Anne. 'I can feel a chill in my bones. I need warming up.'

'I know what you need,' whispered Will, resting a hand on Mary-Anne's thigh.

Mary-Anne shook him off and flapped the reins vigorously. 'Don't you ever learn? I told you to keep your hands to yourself.'

'Once a whore always a whore,' said Will.

Once a fire was lit and coffee brewed – which Mary-Anne found in the cupboard - together with some basic victuals - spirits were generally revived, more so when she produced a half-bottle of liquor from her trunk.

'Right,' said Will. 'Let's see what we've made.'

'OK,' said Jed. 'But first, show me the $50 dollar bill.'

'Are you accusing me…?'

'Nope! I just want to make sure we re-wrap it, proper-like.'

Will fumbled in his pocket and threw the soap and the fifty-dollar bill on the table. 'I'm trusting you, Jed Hansen, the least you can do is trust me.'

''Ain't no need to get riled, Will. We're all friends here.' Jed emptied his pockets and wallet and Will began to count up.

'Two hundred and ten dollars. Not bad for a place like Flint.' He took a small bundle of notes for himself and pushed the rest towards Jed. 'Just do as I say, partners, and this could be the beginning of a beautiful friendship. Yes sir!'

When the time came for sleep Jed suggested Mary-Anne have the box-bed.

'I can't say I take a fancy to it,' said Mary-Anne her nose wrinkling in disgust at the tattered old mattress. 'Looks a little too alive for me. I'll go get some blankets from the wagon.'

'Fine, you take the bed, Will – you being the senior partner and all. Mary-Anne and me, we'll make do on the floor.'

Will knew that calling him the senior partner was no more than a sop to his vanity and it annoyed him. 'Why should you sleep with her?' he said. 'It ain't fair that you should have her. We should share her out. Cheap night for both of us.'

Jed was on Will in seconds. He grabbed his lapels and lifted him off the ground. 'Listen, Penfold. I like your ideas, but that don't mean I like you. As for talking about Mary-Anne like that…we're partners -all three of us - whether you like it or not. She's doing her bit and you show her some respect. You hear me?' Jed shook the slighter man till his head wobbled.

'Sure, Jed. No need to get on your high horse. It was the drink talking that's all. I'm a bit needy, see. I ain't had a woman for….'

'I don't want to know!' hissed Jed. 'Just keep your dirty thoughts to yourself or you'll have me to deal with - and I got a short fuse when it comes to complainin'.'

Mary-Anne, unaware of the confrontation in the cabin, returned with the blankets and made up two beds in front of the stove – one for herself and another for Jed.

The temperature fell dramatically overnight and although all had gone to bed fully dressed Mary-Anne was shivering and with the cold came a desperate need to pee. She got up and went outside. It was very dark and the filtered moonlight offered little help. She kept close to the cabin walls feeling her way round to the back of the cabin. A shaft of moonlight illuminated lit a leaf-strewn patch and, lifting her skirt, she squatted down. The relief of passing water momentarily warmed her then her blood chilled. Between her feet, only partly hidden among the leaves, was a man's face.

A noise, maybe a scream, roused Will from his slumbers. Gun in hand he sat up staring at the cabin door. It was closed. The stove had gone out and as his eyes adjusted to the lack of light he could see that Mary-Anne's bed was empty. His first thought was to see if Jed was still there. He was, and sleeping soundly. Will got up and went outside. He had only taken two or three paces when Mary-Anne flung herself into his arms. Had she been waiting for him? Will's passion was aroused.

'I knew you wanted it,' he whispered, 'You whores are all the same.'

'What? Get off me,' hissed Mary-Anne, struggling to free herself from his grip.

'You little she-dog. You gonna fight me, again? I like a woman with spirit. You know I've wanted you since I first saw you. You and me, we could work this soap swindle together. Just you and me, honey.' He pulled her head back by her thick, red hair and kissed her. 'You and me. We're two of a kind. We take our opportunities where we can.'

He could feel the Mary-Anne's body suddenly relax. 'You are so right,' she whispered. 'We must take every opportunity.'

She pressed her body against his, her right leg around his thigh. He grinned thinking of what was to come, then his head jerked back and the smile disappeared. Even in the pale light Mary-Anne had the satisfaction of seeing his face crease with pain as the cool blade of her stiletto sliced into his heart

SIX

As the life force spilled out of Will's body he slumped to the ground and, because he was still clutching Mary-Anne, he pulled her down too. Realising she may have gone a step too far this time, she quickly distentagled herself from Will's ghoulish embrace. It wasn't her usual practice to kill the goose that laid the golden egg – especially before it had laid it - but Penfold was dispensable. She and Jed could work the soap swindle without him.

Will's body suddenly toppled forwards exposing the slim blade embedded in his back. This sudden movement brought Mary-Anne's thoughts sharply into focus. She pulled out the knife and wiped it clean on Will's jacket and returned it to the small leather pocket stitched inside her boot. Then she grasped his feet and dragged him clear of the cabin. It wasn't too far down to the river, and he rolled most of the way, but before she pushed him into his watery grave, Mary-Anne went through the contents of his pockets.

When she got back she walked Will's horse into the trees and smacked its rear as hard as she could. The startled horse bolted and it was with some satisfaction that Mary-Anne saw it galloping away. Then she went into the cabin and slipped into bed beside Jed. Jed stirred in his sleep, turned towards her and flung his arm across her body.

At sun-up it was obvious there were only two of them.

'Where's Will?' asked Jed.

'Can't say,' said Mary-Anne. 'Outside maybe?'

Jed went to look but was back within seconds. 'His horse has gone. Look's like he's lit out. Now, why would he do that?'

'Who knows?' said Mary-Anne, calmly. 'Coffee, honey?'

Jed began searching Penfold's bed. 'He's taken the money.'

Mary-Anne spun round. 'He's taken *our* money?'

'Well, he ain't taken mine. I tucked my share in my boots last night and I don't take them off for no-one.'

Once Mary-Anne had the coffee-pot on the stove she began shaking her blankets. 'Tarnation!' she cried. 'He's taken my mine too! What are we going to do now?'

Jed sighed. 'Well, my old ma always said it ain't no use crying over spilt milk. And it ain't! I've got enough money to get us started again. But it'll need the two of us. Are you still in, Mary-Anne? 50-50?'

'Sure am! Like I said, I got plans and they ain't no good without money. I say, we can we move on to the next town first thing in the morning.'

Jed gave her a squeeze. 'I knew you wouldn't let me down. But before we go, there's just one thing I got to do.'

'What's that?'

'Well…it's the old timer who used to live here. I dumped him round the back but I'd like to give him a proper burial.'

'Snakes in hell!' said Mary-Anne. '*You* did that? I went outside on a call of nature it near frightened the shit out of me when I squatted down to see his wrinkly face staring up at me.'

Jed laughed. 'I'll bet it did.'

'Where did you find him?'

'Right here in the doorway. Couldn't leave him there. Untidy, and not nice for a little lady to be steppin' over a dead body every time she goes in and out.'

'Did you kill him, Jed?'

'Hell, no. He was dead when I got here.'

Mary-Anne lifted her chin and shrugged. 'You don't say.'

They found a flat piece of ground and, using the miner's tools, Jed dug a fair-sized hole. Together, he and Mary-Anne carried the old timer to the grave and gently lowered him in.

'Ain't no good at prayin',' said Jed when they had re-filled the grave.

'Me neither,' said Mary-Anne. 'Rest in Peace is as good as anything I guess.'

'Yep. Rest in peace old man,' said Jed. 'OK. That's that. Now, if we're moving out, Mary-Anne we'll need water.'

'You see to the horse. I'll go. I'll need some water for washin' too.'

Now, Mary-Anne's prime reason for offering to get the water was to make sure that Will Penfold's body had not got caught up on some rocks or overhanging branches. Thankfully it had not. The river was running swift and clear and the morning sun sparkled like so many diamonds on the fast moving ripples. She was so taken up with the beauty of it all was unaware of Jed's presence until he took her by the shoulders and spun her round.

'So he took off with our money, did he?' Jed's mouth was hard and his eyes narrow and mean.

'Let me go, Jed. You're hurting me.'

Jed gripped her even tighter. 'Will Penfold. What happened, Mary-Anne?'

'I told you what happened.'

Jed twisted her arm behind her back and marched her up to the cabin.

'See that?' he said, pointing at the loaded wagon. 'Now why would Penfold leave his precious stock behind. It don't make sense. And another thing.' He whistled softly and Will's horse trotted out of the trees.

'OK. OK! Let go of me and I'll tell you.'

'Nope. You tell me first!'

'Will Penfold's been pestering me ever since he set eyes on me. Once a whore always a whore, he said. He couldn't keep his hands off me. Like I said, last night I went outside and when I saw that face in the leaves I was up and running faster than you can spit and I ran straight into Will Penfold. He must've heard me go outside and came after me. I tell you Jed he was up my skirts like a weasel on heat and I don't like that. So I killed him.'

'How?'

Mary-Anne showed Jed the knife in her boot. 'A girl's got to have some protection.'

'Where is he now?'

'In the river.'

Jed was momentarily lost for words experiencing, as he was, a barrel-full of mixed emotions. On the one hand he had nothing but admiration for Mary-Anne's courage and sense of self preservation, on the other a frisson of fear that she was one mighty dangerous animal to be bedding down with.

'Right,' he said, releasing his hold on her, 'and his share of the money? What happened to that?'

Mary-Anne tilted her head and gave Jed a wry smile. Then she lifted her skirts and removed a small silk purse from her garter, dangling it in front of him.

'Well, I guess that's that. We've buried one corpse and you've gotten rid of the other. As far as I can see there's nuthin' more to do. We'd best get on the road again.'

'A kiss to seal the new partnership?' said Mary-Anne.

Gone was the ice-cool murderess, Mary-Anne was looking up at him coquettish and kitten-like, her lips parted seductively. He knew he was going to have his hands full with this woman and he would have to keep a close watch on her - but how exciting was that going to be? He was already addressing the fact that he was actually looking forward to it.

Jed drew her towards him and as their lips touched he took her hands and placed them round his neck, at the same time removing the silk money purse and slipping it into his back pocket.

SEVEN

Over the coming months and on into the Fall, Jed and Mary-Anne travelled North through Utah and into Idaho, playing the soap game with continued success although not without difficulties. There was an occasion in Eureka, Idaho that all but landed him in jail.

The soap was selling well when a young boy in the crowd shouted out, 'Save your money. There ain't no $100 bills. It's a swindle. He works it with another man in the crowd. I live in Spanish Fort and he was there not two days back. My ma paid $10 for a 2-bit bar of soap and she got nuthin'.'

The boy's words were having the desired effect on the crowd. Some began to back away.

'I can assure you, ladies and gentlemen,' said Jed, 'this boy is mistaken.'

At this point Mary-Anne, standing nearby said, 'I'll take one, mister!'

'Why thank you ma-am,' says Jed, handing her the bar containing the $25 bill.'

While the crowd watched Mary-Anne unwrapped the soap and with a cry held the bill aloft. 'Twenty five dollars!' she screamed. 'It ain't no trick. Give me another one mister!'

The crowd was satisfied and started buying again but the boy ran off. Jed was glad to see the back of him but he returned a few minutes later accompanied by a thick-set, hard-nosed man with his thumbs tucked into his gunbelt.

'Hey!' cried the boy, waving his arms. 'This here's my pa!' But they were too busy buying and nobody paid any attention so the man drew both his guns and fired into the air. Some of the women, especially those with babies in their arms, screamed and ran for shelter. The rest of the crowd looked round to see what all the shooting was about.

The boy spoke first. 'My pa says that man's a killer and my Pa's a marshal.'

'That's right,' said the man, exposing the badge on his waistcoat. 'I know who you are. You're a murderer, a swindler and a thief and I've been on your trail since you crossed into Idaho.'

'Why, sir,' said Jed, all smiles and charm, 'you must be thinking of somebody else.'

Mary-Anne was already up in the driving seat and gathering the reins. 'Quit the fancy talk, Jed," she hissed, ' and let's get out of here! I told you it was too close to our last job.'

'Oh, it's you all right,' said the marshal, 'I got your picture here! 'And he held up a very crumpled and badly printed 'wanted' poster. 'See that, folks! Ain't that him?'

Unable to resist, Mary-Anne turned round to have a look. 'Hell's bells! It sure does look like you but it's Soapy Smith. I seen that poster before. Hold tight. Time to go.'

Mary-Anne slapped the reins and Jed, standing on the backboard, all but fell off as the wagon lurched forward.

'Don't let them get away!' yelled the marshal. 'You men! You're all deputies. Get your horses and follow me.'

Jed climbed into the driver's seat beside Mary-Anne. 'Keep low,' he said, as they rattled out of town. The old horse, under extreme pressure from Mary-Anne, was doing its best to make speed over the boulder-strewn track but it was not good enough.

'They'll catch us up at this rate,' said Jed. 'I'll have to set up a diversion. Follow the track, Mary-Anne, straight on into the hills and keep driving as hard as you can.'

While Mary Anne whipped the weary beast to within an inch of it's life Jed clambered to the rear of the wagon where his and Will Penfold's horses were hitched. He undid the reins of Will's horse and dragged it forward retying it beside Mary-Anne.

'What the hell are you doing?' screamed Mary-Anne. 'You ain't fixing on leaving me, are you?'

'Shut up and do as I say,' said Jed, falling into the seat beside her. ' Give me the reins and get off!'

'What?'

'Take Will's horse and go. I'll drive on.' They could hear the rumble of several horses behind them and some random shots. 'Hell, Mary-Anne, what are you waitin' for?'   Ahead and rising up into the distance were the mountains and to the left a worn track that wound its way down to the valley below. 'Down there!' yelled Jed. 'Hole-up down there somewhere. I'll find you later.'

Hanging on to the driver's seat with one hand, Mary-Anne tried to straddle the horse but her dress was caught round the brake handle.

'Darned skirt!' she cried, ripping it free and tucking it her lace-trimmed drawers.

Jed grinned. 'Mighty fancy outfit, ma-am.'

'You keep your eyes up front!' shouted Mary-Anne, as she leapt into the bouncing saddle then, 'Holy cow!' as she connected with the horn.

'Cut the lead rein,' yelled Jed, 'and keep to the track.'

Mary-Anne, swearing like a trouper, took the knife from her boot and cut the rein that tied the horse to the wagon. Sheathing the knife she then allowed the excited animal its head. Jed watched them both disappear between the rocks in a cloud of dust, down into the darkness and out of sight.

He could hear the posse getting ever closer. He reined in the horse, did a quick turnabout to cover Mary-Anne's tracks, and then rode off down the steeper, rougher side of the mountain in the opposite direction.

Although it was unknown territory he drove between the rocks with reckless speed and little regard for his safety. A bullet screamed past and ricocheted off the rocks then another. It was too close for comfort but it gave Jed the satisfaction of knowing that the posse was on *his* trail and not Mary-Anne's. Then, something exploded in his right shoulder sending a searing burst of pain through his body, a pain that sliced through his bones and screamed in his brain.

The Marshal and his posse came to an abrupt halt, and watched in satisfied silence, as the wagon went over the edge. They saw it hurtling over the rocks with the unfortunate horse still between the shafts but no driver for Jed's body had already been flung out. For a while the noise was horrendous. The sharp, pistol-like sounds of splintering wood and the gut-wrenching cries of the injured horse echoed round the mountainside for several minutes. Then there was silence.

'OK men!' said the marshal, 'Let's go. That's the last we'll see of him.'

EIGHT

Jed woke up feeling warm and relaxed except for a grinding headache. He stretched his legs. He was in bed. But whose bed and where? He opened his eyes. He was in a roughly built log cabin with a large, central chimney-stack. The cabin was unkempt and dirty but the clothes on his bed looked clean enough. There was very little furniture in the room and what there was had seen better days. On the other side of the stack he could see the edge of a simple table made from split logs. Immediately to his left, just a pace away, was a dust-covered window. The floor around the bed was strewn with trash of all kinds, empty bottles, shoes, paper, some clothes and a few large furs – bear or maybe polecat. He guessed this had once been a trapper's cabin and the long-barrelled plains rifle fixed over the doorway confirmed it.

Then the door opened and a woman of indeterminate age and shape came in. She was broad-shouldered and muscular and was carrying an armful of logs but was wearing a low cut, red-satin dress several sizes too small. Ripples of compressed flesh were desperately trying to escape from the split seams and her breasts were forced upwards and outwards by the tightly laced, high-boned bodice. She took no notice of Jed but dropped the logs onto the hearth.

'Excuse me," said Jed. 'Where am I?'

'Oh? So you're awake,' she said, turning towards the bed. 'Does your lickle wound feel better now?' She spoke in a childish, singsong voice, which did not suit the square jawed and grubby face or the painted mouth from which it came.

'Thank you, yes,' said Jed, attempting to sit up, but his nurse pushed him back with a firm hand.

'Not time for baby to get up! Did you know you had a nasty bullet in your shoulder? Betsy got it out for you. Betsy good nurse.'

'I'm obliged,' said Jed. 'Exactly how long have I been here?'

'Oh, two maybe three days. You hit your poor head badly. You was unconscious when I found you and you been that way ever since. But Betsy make you better.' She tucked in the bedclothes in with a vigour that made Jed cry out in pain.

'That's real good of you,' he said, through gritted teeth. 'I thank you kindly but I feel fine now and I'd like to get up.'

There was a mean, scolding look in the large woman's eyes as she held her patient down – this time with both hands.

'Naughty boy! You can't get up yet because your clothes ain't dry.'

Clothes? Jed raised the sheet and looked down at his naked body. Betsy was grinning like a kid who'd found the candy jar and Jed felt his pulse quicken as embarrassment and panic washed over him. He was beginning to think that the addle-brained Betsy had some kind of ulterior motive for keeping him in bed. This woman may well have saved his life with her ministrations but she blatantly wanted more for her trouble and, if he guessed right, it wasn't the kind of payment he was prepared to give.

'Look ma-am, you've been very kind but...'

'Ma-am!' she shrieked, clapping her large hands. 'Ain't nobody called me that in years. Guess you must like me, mister. Am I right?'

Before Jed could think of an acceptable answer the door opened again and a small boy, maybe eight or nine years, came in. He was dirty and poorly dressed in a pair of faded and ragged dungarees. He stood in the doorway, head bent, staring down at his bare feet.

'You keep out of here, dirty Toomey,' says Betsy angrily, waving her arm in his direction. 'Can't you see I'm entertainin'?'

The boy looked up. His face was almost expressionless but Jed reckoned he saw something akin to desperation in the boy as their eye's met. He also noticed the bruising around the boy's forehead.

'You go see to the chickens, Toomey,' said Betsy. 'One of 'em needs killing. And chop some wood for the stove. I don't want to see you lazing about doin' nuthin'. But if I do - you'll be punished and you know how good I am at that! Now git!'

As soon as the boy had gone Betsy collapsed into peals of laughter.

'He's scared of me,' she said, 'and that's how I like it. I was raped, see and he was the result. Didn't want him! No sir!' She shrugged her shoulders and her up-thrust breasts wobbled grotesquely. 'But nor did anybody else, so I've been saddled with him ever since.'

While she was prattling on Jed was thinking about how he'd come to be here with this strange woman. He couldn't remember much and, if he was unconscious when she found him, he must have been in a bad state. But what else did she find? His money? Jed suddenly recalled having a good stash of money. He had stored the bulk of it in his saddle-bag but had carried a few hundred dollars in his jacket and boots.

'My clothes, ma-am? Where are my clothes?'

Betsy pointed to the window. 'Drying in the sun. See? I washed 'em with my new soap. I found lots and lots of it and all neatly wrapped. Jesus must've sent that down for me 'cos *He* knows how much washing I do. Now I won't have to make no soap for maybe a year or more.'

Jed raised his head sufficiently to see, through the dirt on the window, his jacket and pants spread out on some boulders a few yards away from the cabin.

'Why they look good and dry to me. Maybe I could take a look.' He started to sit up.

'No!' She turned and looked at him angrily with wild, staring eyes. 'Only Betsy go look. You stay here. It's Betsy's washing. Betsy good at washing. She used to be the best but nobody to wash for now.' Then she smiled and the manic grin looked even more disturbing than the anger. 'But I washed you good. Head to toe. Every little bit of you and I gave you a shave.'

Jed rubbed his chin in amazement. His cheeks felt smooth and soft just like a woman's.

'Betsy good with razor, yes?'

Jed sensed a compliment was required. 'Best shave I ever had.'

She seemed happy with that and sat down on the bed, digging her long fingers into his legs and giggling like an overgrown baby who knew it was doing something very naughty. Then just when her probing fingers were getting worryingly close to Jed's groin she stopped abruptly, stood up and twirled round. 'You like my new dress?'

Jed knew that if he was to get anywhere with this crazy woman he had to humour her. 'Sure do, ma-am. You look as pretty as a bride.'

But that was not what she wanted to hear. Once again the angry face, the screwed-up piggy eyes. 'Ain't never been a bride," she snapped.

'Could've been! Would've liked a husband to wash for. Did you know men used to fight over me? But after Toomey nobody wanted me. I was a dirty Betsy.' And she spat on the floor.

'Have you got any kinfolk around here?' asked Jed, desperately trying to change the subject.

'Why you asking all these questions? None of your business. Betsy's business. Anyway ain't got none. Ain't got nobody.'

'What about the boy?' suggested Jed.

'He ain't mine!' she said fiercely. 'He was put inside me against my will by that pig Toomey. I didn't want him and I don't want him now. But nobody will take him off me.' Her mood changed abruptly and she said softly, 'Would you like to take him mister?' But before Jed could answer Betsy said sharply. 'Silly Betsy. Of course you can't because you ain't going nowhere. You're staying here with me.'

'Well,' said Jed, 'If'n I'm staying, I'd like to be decent, ma-am and get some clothes on.'

'You can get dressed when I'm ready for you to get dressed,' she said sternly. 'Now Betsy will fix you something nice to eat. I've got some chicken stew needs eatin'.'

He could hear her rattling pans and fussing about on the other side of the chimney. It was then Jed had a vision of somebody else wearing that dress. Somebody leaning on the bar in front of him, smiling up at him and looking good enough to eat. Mary-Anne! His memory came flooding back. The two of them were being chased by a posse. She took off down one side of the mountain and he….? He recalled being tossed out of the wagon and falling but after that – nothing. He sat up wincing at the pain in his shoulder and his sore and bloodied head.

In a corner of the room, part-hidden by the clutter that surrounded it, he could see something familiar. Mary-Anne's trunk. 'So,' he thought, 'Mad Betsy must have found that too.'

A shadow fell across the bed from the window. Jed looked up and saw the boy Toomey signalling to Jed to come closer. Taking a sheet from the bed to cover his nakedness Jed stood up. It was only when he was upright that he realised how weak he was. His legs felt like Jell-O.

'What is it?' he whispered, his face as close to the smeared glass as he dared.

The boy was also whispering and Jed could not properly make out what he was saying but it seemed as though he was offering to get Jed's clothes for him.

'That'd be great but I can't get out of here. The door's locked. Your mother has the key and this window is nailed up.'

'I'll get you out,' said the boy, 'if you promise to take me with you.'

'Oh, I'm not sure. I mean your mother...'

'Please, mister. She don't want me. I won't be no trouble. I've found your horse but she don't know it yet. I hid it.'

That was good news indeed and it helped Jed to come to a decision. 'OK!' he hissed. 'Help me get out and it's a deal. '

Jed suddenly became aware of a strange silence. Betsy had stopped singing. He slid back into the bed and pulled the covers up to his chin. He checked the window but the boy had gone.

Betsy came in carrying in a tray of food. 'I thought I heard you talking? Who you bin talking to?'

'Oh, that was me singing, ma-am. Never was very good at it.'

'So you're feeling better then?'

'Oh yes, ma-am.'

'Huh!' She frowned. She did not look too pleased to hear this. 'Now you sit up. Betsy made this fine stew.' She placed a tray on Jed's lap and plumped the pillow behind him. 'Now you eat while Betsy go out. Betsy needs to go pee-pee and pooh-pooh.'

The stew looked dubious but smelled good and Jed, whose stomach was fair groaning for sustenance, wasn't feeling too fussy. Betsy waited while he sampled her stew and had offered suitable grunts of approval, before she left. She left in a hurry, slamming the door which bounced in the frame. Within seconds Toomey was inside the cabin.

'Hey mister! I got your clothes. She was in such a darned hurry she forgot to lock the door. She's gone down to her special place and she'll be there a while. She goes at this time every day.'

Toomey threw Jed's jacket and pants onto the bed.

'Thanks boy.' Jed was grateful but dressing with his injuries was not so easy. Toomey, meanwhile, was twitchy and nervous and running back to the door. 'Hurry up mister. Jest get your pants on. The rest can wait.'

Jed's clothes had shrunk with the washing and were hard baked by the sun. The pants were as stiff as two boards and about as comfortable. Even so he dragged them on.

'Where's my boots?'

'She threw' 'em away, or hid 'em. Couldn't find 'em.'

Cursing at the loss of his boots, Jed first of all checked that the money was still in his jacket and hallelujah, it was! It had suffered a bit with Betsy's washing but it was all there!

'Come on, mister. We're wasting time.'

Outside and away from the cabin the boy was like a young goat hopping and leaping over the boulders and rocks but Jed, struggling with soft, bare feet and injuries, was not half as nimble. Eventually, Toomey led him up the mountain to a large overhang that partially hid the entrance to a huge cave. It was pitch black inside but Jed could smell the horse even before he saw it. He felt for its nose and it whinnied its welcome. Then Jed's hands travelled down its neck to the saddle and the saddlebag. That too was as he had left it. Unopened.

'Thanks, Toomey,' he said, patting the boy's head. 'You done real well. What happened to the wagon? '

'That was all broke up and the horse was dead when I found it. But there was soap everywhere. Betsy had that. She didn't know about this horse because it ran off, but I found it later.'

'You're a good boy, Toomey." He struggled into the crisp, stiff shirt and sun-bleached jacket. 'OK. We're ready to move out.'

With the boy up behind him, Jed urged his horse up the mountainside heading east.

'This ain't the way out,' cried the boy, tugging at Jed's jacket. 'We'll pass above the cabin. She'll see us and she's a mean shot with the rifle.'

'Maybe, but there's somethin' I got to do,' said Jed, grimly. 'Before the accident I left my partner on the other side of this mountain and I got to see if she's OK.'

The sound of a rifle shot echoed round their ears and the horse stumbled. Toomey grasped Jed even tighter. 'She's seen us, mister.'

More shots, this time from a repeater, ricocheted off the rocks accompanied by Betsy's frantic screams from below. Jed coaxed the frightened horse ever higher and as the angle got steeper and the horse less sure-footed, he could feel Toomey's grip slackening.

'Hold on tight, boy,' he said. 'We'll soon be out of range.'

By the time they reached the top the firing had ceased. Jed could only guess how angry Betsy would be but that was too bad. It was no way to carry on holding a man like that and taking all his clothes. He quickly found the track where he and Mary-Anne had parted.

'You're free now, boy,' he said, looking over his shoulder at Toomey whose head was resting on Jed's back. As he turned the boy slid off the horse and fell to the ground. Jed immediately jumped down beside him. 'What's up? You unwell, boy?'

But there was no answer. One of Betsy's bullets had struck home and caught Toomey in the back. The boy was dead.

NINE

Jed could not believe the boy's appalling luck. He'd had a terrible start in life, unwanted and unloved and just when he had the opportunity to get away make something of his life, he was struck down. It near broke Jed's heart to see the boy lying there, pale and lifeless. He hardly knew why should it matter so much but it did. The boy had had a rough deal in life through no fault of his own.

Jed found a patch of fairly soft ground behind some large rocks and scraped out a shallow grave using some stones. It took him a while, and brought him out in a sweat but he needed to do it - not only for Toomey - but also for himself. It helped to suppress feelings that were dangerously close to the surface. After an hour or so of scratching and digging Jed went back for Toomey, and carried him over to the grave. He'd thought nothing of burying the old miner. Somebody else had shot him and he was doing him a service but this was different. This boy didn't deserve to die. Shovelling the dirt over Toomey's face was more than Jed could bear and he was unable to suppress his emotions. When he'd done he placed a pile of rocks at the head of the grave to mark the spot. Then he turned abruptly and remounted his horse.

As he rode further down into the valley his thoughts returned to Mary-Anne. He did not think she would be there but he had to look. She'd have more sense than to wait around for a no-good drifter like himself to turn up. Anything could have happened. The marshal could have caught him; he could have been shot. Even so he still looked for signs of a camp or a fire. It was deathly silent at the bottom of the valley. Along by the river the trees grew close together and let in very little light and what there was rapidly fading. Jed was obliged to give up his search.

It may have been coming right on top of Toomey's death but the loss of Mary-Anne's company, and indeed Toomey's, made Jed feel pretty low. He rode on through the valley and up across the mountain. It was too dark to do any more looking and he didn't much feel like going any further till daylight so he decided to bed down and start again in the morning. A new day, a new start - even a new life.

He untied his bedroll, spread the paulin on the ground with his blanket on top. The temperature had already dropped and, without boots, he was more than ready to curl up and go to sleep. Before he settled down he hitched the horse to a tree then, with his gun in his hand, lay down and wrapped himself up in the blanket pulling it right over his head.

A noise, he couldn't say what, woke him up. It was still dark and he lay unmoving, his ears alert for further noise or movement nearby. A twig cracked underfoot as somebody approached and then the blanket was gingerly drawn back from his face.

'Is he dead?'

So there was more than one of them thought Jed.

'Could be,' said a voice, 'could be sick, but by the way he's wrapped up looks to me like somebody meant to bury him.' A boot prodded Jed in the buttocks. 'He ain't movin'.' Jed felt the barrel of a rifle poking the small of his back. 'Shall I give him a shot, Abe, just to make sure.'

'What fer? He ain't gonna trouble no one if he's dead. Search him, Luke. See if he's anything worth stealin'.'

But before Luke could investigate the blanket was flung back and, quick as a snake and twice as deadly, Jed Hansen was on his feet both guns drawn. To his surprise he faced two young hillbilly's whose wide-eyed paralysis gave Jed precious seconds in which to fire. Luke, the shorter and younger, screamed as he dropped the rifle and grasped his bloodied hand.

'What you done that fer?' he cried. 'My pa'll have your hide!'

'You were going to shoot me!' said Jed.

'Wouldn't have hurt none 'cos we thought you was dead!'

'But I ain't.'

'No harm done, mister,' said the one called Abe, raising his hands, 'my young cousin here's a bit frisky like. Out looking for rabbits and it's the first time I let him carry the rifle.'

'Throw down your guns,' said Jed. 'Over here, by me - and real easy.'

Abe removed a pistol from the waistband of his pants and tossed it at Jed's feet. Jed picked it up. 'And you!' He indicated the moaning Luke who was still nursing his wounded hand.

'He don't have no gun,' said his cousin.

'OK, but keep your hands above your head where I can see them.'

Luke, obsessed by his injury, ignored Jed's command.

'Do as he says,' hissed Abe.

Reluctantly, Luke held up his hands. 'But, cousin, all the blood'll run out of my hand.'

"Shut up,' said Abe.

'Now listen up,' said Jed. 'I've a mind to make a bargain with you.'

Luke immediately started protesting. 'We don't bargain with nobody. Don't listen to him, Cousin Abe. He hurt me bad. He could'a killed me.'

'Shut up, will ya. What sort of bargain mister?'

Still keeping a cautious eye on the two young men, Jed walked over to his horse. He holstered one gun as he slipped the tie-rope off his saddle - turning away only for a split second - but it was time enough for Abe to make a lunge for the forgotten rifle. Jed, seeing the movement out of the corner of his eye, fired at the dirt under Abe's feet. The long-legged Abe leaped into the air like a giant grasshopper, clutching his foot and cursing profusely.

'Goddammit, you sonofabitch! What you do that fer?'

Abe!' cried Luke, running over, 'are you hurt!'

'God dammit! O 'course I'm hurt. He darned near shot my foot off!'

'Oh Jesus!' cried Luke. 'There's a hole clean through the toe of your boot. That'll let water in and you'll get pnuemony.'

'Never mind the puemony, get my darned boot off. I've been shot!'

'Sorry, cousin, just thinking aloud!'

'And when did you ever think, you lam-brained idiot!'

Jed could see these two were a pair of simple mountain folk and possibly no real threat – although Luke had been ready enough to shoot him when he had the chance. He reflected then that mad Betsy had also been a bit trigger-happy. Maybe living in these mountains made folk loco. He looped the rope around their wrists and tied their hands together behind their backs. Then he tied their feet.

'You ain't gonna leave us here like this?' howled Luke. 'We're injured. We could bleed to death. I don't want to die here, Cousin Abe.'

'For the love of Christ, will you stop whining!' shouted Abe. 'We ain't two miles from home. Someone will come and find us afore nightfall.' And then to Jed, 'So what's this here bargain, mister?'

'Well, I ain't gonna kill you, though I could if I had mind to since you tried to kill me, but you happen to have something I need.'

'We ain't got nuthin', mister,' cried Luke. You can search us if'n you like.'

Jed surveyed the soiled and ill-fitting pants they were wearing and the sweat-drenched armpits of their jackets and was grateful for the fact that a search was unnecessary. 'No need. I want your boots.' Both Abe and Luke's eyes drifted down to Jed's bare feet.

'How come you ain't got none?' asked Luke.

'It's a long story,' said Jed, 'and I've no mind to be telling it right now.'

Jed guessed Abe's feet were about the same size as his own but his boots were terribly misshapen and the left one had the blood-stained bullet-hole. So, it had to be Luke's. But when he removed them the smell of sour, unwashed feet seeping out was stomach churning and Jed was mighty relieved to find they were too small. So Abe's boots it had to be but they were no sweeter than his cousins and darned uncomfortable. Abe must have had one leg longer than the other because the left boot had a much thicker sole. Once shod, Jed unhitched his horse and left the pair of them sitting on the ground arguing and cursing. As Abe had said, they weren't far from home and it would be sun up soon. They'd be OK.

After another cold night on the mountain Jed was relieved to find a decent sort of town on the other side. Desperate though he was for a long cool beer, the matter of some new boots was even more pressing. The proprietor of 'The Finest Boots in Town' (as the sign proclaimed) was only too happy to assist. 'Yes sir. Sit down sir and I will measure your feet. Oh dear me. What's this? I see you have had a nasty accident, sir,'

'Yep, stray bullet,' said Jed.

The bootmaker nodded but made no further comment. He measured Jed's foot and then showed him a variety of boots. 'Made from the finest, the supplest, the very best calfskin. Note the decorative motif at the top sir.'

'Yep. These'll do,' said Jed, after trying on the first pair.

Having settled his bill, and with the old boots left behind, Jed then found a room in a small boarding house on the opposite side of the street. He hardly recognized the dishevelled hobo that stared back from the mirror in his room. His unkempt hair was greasy and lank, he had six or seven days growth of unruly beard and his clothes, though clean after Betsy's vigorous washing, were fit for nothing but the fire.

But the main priority was a long hot soak in the tub – a privilege for which he had to negotiate hard. The owner of the boarding house, a respectable matron of some fifty summers or more, was not happy with idea of this stranger bathing in her back kitchen. However, generous terms were agreed and Jed was supplied with a tin bath, a bar of soap and several kettles of hot water. After a good long soak in front of the range, he dressed and went out to look around the town. It was a well-established and seemingly thriving place with every sort of store a body could need. Apart from the bootmaker there was a Livery Stables, a General Store and Thompson's Tonsorial Parlour. Jed treated himself to a shave and a haircut by Mr Thompson after which he felt half decent enough to go into Svenson's Clothing Store and buy himself a new out-fit.

'Can I help you, sir?' said a rather frail-looking, grey moustachioed man standing behind the counter and whom Jed surmised to be Mr Svenson himself.

'You can indeed,' said Jed. 'Tell me, what is the name of this town?'

'Why this here's Bolterstown,' came the reply, 'on account of Henry Bolter, the man who founded it.'

'Is that so,' said Jed. 'And what State is it in?'

Mr Svenson, if indeed that was he, gave Jed a sideways glance. 'Don't you know?'

'No sir. Been riding hard these last few days - as you can probably tell by the state of my clothes. This here's my first stop.'

'You're not, excuse me asking sir,' Jed noticed the old man's hands were trembling, 'you're not running from the law by any chance?'

'Why no, indeed I ain't,' said Jed, conferring one of his brilliant smiles on the nervous old man. 'It's a long story, and I know I look a mess, but I got badly injured in a fall and was laid up for several days. Lost part of my memory. Can't remember where I'm going or where I've been.'

'Oh that's terrible bad. I'm so sorry, sir. Well, right now you are in Washington State.'

'Never heard of it,' said Jed. 'I kinda thought I might be in Oregon Country.'

'Yes, sir, you are. This here was Oregon Country until nine years ago when we became the 42nd State of the United States of America.' The little man beamed at Jed and looked as proud of the fact as if he had been personally involved.

'I didn't know that,' said Jed. 'Like I said. I've been travelling. Not from these parts at all.'

'Well, to give you an idea of where you are, Bolterstown is about 50 miles or so south of Tacoma and that ain't far from Seattle. I'm told there's a lot of gold hunters on their way through Seattle. There's been another gold strike in the Yukon. Is that why you're here?'

Jed shook his head. 'No. I'm here to buy some shirts, a good leather jacket and some hard-wearing pants.'

'Oh yes, sir. Of course sir.' The little man disappeared behind some huge bolts of cloth returning a few minutes later with the requisite clothing and more conversation. 'Of course Seattle ain't what it was when I was a young man. Burned to a cinder it was just ten years ago. All rebuilt. Would you like me to wrap these for you, sir.'

'No thanks,' said Jed. 'Is there's somewhere I can try them on?'

'Of course, of course. This way, sir.'

Although he probably meant well, and was trying to be friendly, Jed found the old man's prattle intrusive and irritating beyond measure and he could not get out of the store quickly enough. The old man had offered to dispose of Jed's old clothes for which he was grateful. He felt much better in his new duds, and his fancy calfskin boots made a satisfying click on the sidewalk as he walked towards the saloon. It was called The Alhambra and sounded promising. Jed had a vision of a crusty meat pie with lashings of gravy washed down with a cool beer followed by a few slugs of whiskey and, maybe, some female entertainment. As he crossed the road he heard a sharp metallic click from behind which made him turn - hand on gun. But it was only the old storekeeper, locking up his shop. Jed watched him scuttling along the boardwalk to the bootmaker's shop. There was something about the furtive way the old man looked around before entering the shop that made Jed frown. Something going on?

'Hell,' he told himself, 'think of that pie and beer. Whatever's going on, it ain't got nothin' to do with you.'

As soon as he entered The Alhambra Jed's spirits rose. He stood there for a moment drinking in the undefined but heightened atmosphere that pervaded such establishments and usually spelled out a good time. The honky-tonk piano was churning out a tune and there were plenty of card games in progress. He considered trying to get in on one but later, after he'd had a drink or two. He eased his way to the front of the crowded bar but it was some time before he could attract the attention of the barman.

'Hey, Joe. A jug of beer,' shouted Jed. The barman acknowledged his request with a nod of the head but did nothing about it. 'Hey, Joe! You deaf or somethin'? What's a guy got to do to get served around here?'

Jed was suddenly and uncomfortably aware of the press of bodies around him. Then a voice behind him said, 'We don't want no trouble, mister.'

'I ain't giving no trouble,' said Jed. 'I only want a beer.' He tried to turn round to face the speaker but was firmly pinned against the bar rail.

'You done shot the Catchpole boys and we don't tolerate that.'

'You got the wrong man,' said Jed. 'I only just got here.'

'You shot Abe Catchpole and his cousin Luke,' said the voice, 'two innocent boys, and left them to die up on the mountain.'

'So that's who they were? Well, let me tell you, those so-called innocent boys tried to kill me. I snicked the hand of one of them, in self-defence, and grazed the other's toe. They ain't exactly gonna die from that.'

'That ain't what they told me.'

'And who are you anyway?' Jed squeezed round to face his accuser and looked straight into the beady eyes of the bootmaker.

'I'm Abe's Uncle, Josiah Catchpole. I recognized Abe's boots the minute I saw them. Abe's got one leg shorter than the other, see, and I made those boots special. Abe never takes them off. Never! I knew something was up as soon as I saw you. I knew you must have stole 'em to get 'em.'

'How come you're so darned sure it was me?' asked Jed.

'Because the boys came straight to me and told me what happened. They told me you ambushed them, took their guns and tied them up. Left poor Abe with a bullet wound in his foot. They guessed you'd be coming into town and when you did, they pointed you out to me.'

'So they ain't *that* dead,' said Jed.

'No thanks to you, mister. A man can die of gangrene from an untreated bullet wound.'

'But he didn't. And it was just a scratch.'

'Quit arguing with me, will you? Just get on your horse and get out of here. Ain't nothin' for you here.'

'And I've had better welcomes,' said Jed.

Josiah Catchpole stood back to allow Jed to pass but at that moment the saloon doors opened and the lean and barefooted figure of Abe Catchpole limped in. He hobbled over to Jed, his injured toe swathed in bandages, his trembling hands poised over his guns. Those standing at the bar moved to one side. Conversation ceased and all eyes were on Abe. The pianist, who had his back to the action, continued to play for a while until he realised something was going on and then he stopped abruptly.

'Out of my way, Abe,' said Jed, wearily. 'I ain't looking for no fight.'

'But I am,' said Abe, hawking and spitting with considerable expertise into a cuspidor at Jed's feet. 'You took advantage of me and my cousin, just 'cos we're mountain folk. It's time you learned a lesson, mister. Nobody messes with the Catchpoles and gets away with it.'

'Abe!' warned his Uncle. 'It's over. He's leavin'. Let it be.'

'No!' shouted Abe. 'I won't. He yumiliated me in front of my kin!'

'Shoot him, Abe!' shouted Luke, thumping the table and stamping his feet. 'Shoot him like a dog. We should'a done that in the first place. You know I wanted to.'

'Shut your big mouth, Luke!' Abe glared angrily at his cousin and at that moment Jed fired. Abe collapsed on the floor and all hell broke loose.

TEN

Jed found an unexpected ally in Pat O'Reilly, the Bolterstown Marshal, a stocky thick-set man with a furrowed, careworn face that looked as though it had never smiled. According to O'Reilly the Catchpole cousins had been robbing unwary travellers and local farmers for some time but, protected as they were by their large and close-knit family ever ready to provide an alibi, the law had been unable to pin anything on them. When Josiah Catchpole and an assortment of relatives dragged Jed into his office the marshal asked no questions but simply slapped the handcuffs on him, removed his guns and locked him up.

'Don't I get a say?' protested Jed as he was flung into a cell.

'Later.'

'He needs stringing up,' cried Luke, 'You make sure of that, marshal. He's killed my kith and kin.'

'He ain't done nuthin' of the sort,' said O'Reilly pushing the protesting Luke back into the outer office. 'I had a good look at Abe Catchpole in the saloon and, apart from the fact he'd passed out, he ain't bled enough to fill a whiskey glass. Now get out of here, all of you, or I'll put everyone of you in jail for wasting my time.'

As soon as the office was empty, and the outer door closed, Marshal O'Reilly returned to Jed's cell and let him out.

'Sorry about that, mister,' he said. 'It ain't the way we treat all newcomers, you understand, but it was for your own safety. Them Catchpoles is up to all sorts of tricks. They breed like vermin, cunning as rattlesnakes and twice as poisonous. Some of them are right loco too. Take young Betsy Catchpole. You wouldn't want to spend no time with her, believe me. Man mad. Had a child some years back but she don't trouble nobody.'

Jed wondered whether to tell O'Reilly about Toomey. That the boy was dead and where he was buried but he immediately thought better of it. Wouldn't do no good. If the Catchpole family got to know about Toomey he'd likely be accused of killing him.

'If it weren't for the law stepping in,' continued O'Reilly, 'those Catchpoles would ruin this town in no time. They've got some kind of still operating in the mountains and they try selling their coffin varnish to any who'll buy it. One of these days I'm gonna catch 'em out and put 'em all behind bars. That's what helps me sleep at night.' He handed Jed back his guns. 'You aiming to stay here a while?'

'No way. I was heading for The Klondike.'

'Well, good luck, mister. We get a lot of gold hunters passing through Bolterstown and the dregs that comes with 'em. Card sharps, Bunco men, all manner of cheats and swindlers, wanted men, outlaws – keeps me on my toes. Likely them scheming Catchpoles thought you'd got a price on your head.'

'I wonder, have you seen this man?' Jed took out the crumpled and faded wanted poster that he'd carried with him since Oregon. O'Reilly instantly recognized him.

'You want to steer clear of him, mister.'

'You know him?'

'Who doesn't? That's Soapy Smith. One of the slickest swindlers you ever met. He was here in Bolterstown last year, just long enough to remove several hundred dollars from the townsfolk - all took in by his sweet-talk.'

'Even the Catchpoles?'

'Huh! They were the worst. Always looking to make a cheap buck that family, but Soapy was too smart for them hillbillies.'

Jed put the poster back in his pocket. 'I heard he'd set himself up in Skagway?'

'That's right. What's your interest in him, mister?'

'Oh, it's personal. He cheated me a while ago, big time, and I mean to get my money back.'

'Well, that's your affair but let me tell you, he ain't nobody to mess with. He's dangerous. Them Catchpoles is chicken feed compared to Soapy.'

It was dark when Jed left Bolterstown on his way to Seattle. He had a long, hard ride ahead of him but his spirits were high. Marshal O'Reilly had told him there were regular sailings from Seattle to Skagway and that was where he would finally catch up with Smith.

Seattle, the main stopping off point for miners going to the Klondike, was a town possessed and obsessed by gold fever. Some chose to make the long journey overland but others, hundreds of them, hung around on the docks trying to get a ticket for the next boat to Skagway.

After leaving his horse at the livery stables, Jed went straight down to the docks. It was packed solid. Men were pressed shoulder to shoulder some standing right up to the water's edge while others sat on the stacked packing cases and cargo. *The Queen*, a large sail and steamboat, was in the port and was already jam-packed with men. They were four or five deep on the decks and crushed against the railings. They filled the upper decks, the companionways and any other space they could find. Jed could see the boat was lying fairly low in the water but still they were boarding. He made his way, with some difficulty, through the waiting crowd towards the booking office.

'Sorry. Sold out!' said the clerk, when he got there. 'No more tickets today.'

'When's the next sailing?' asked Jed.

'This time next week on *The Empress* - that's if she gets back in one piece.'

'What do you mean by that?'

'Lost a few ships on this route, mister. Dangerous waters. Lots of ice. You pays your money and you takes your chance.'

There was no way Jed was going to wait another two weeks. He pushed his way back through the crush of bodies towards the gangplank. But the patience of the waiting travellers was wearing thin.

'Who d'you think you're shovin' mister?' A broad-shouldered, brute of a miner blocked Jed's path. 'Get back and wait your turn like the rest of us.'

'You got a ticket?' asked Jed.

'What's it to you?'

'Look,' said Jed. 'I've got to get to Skagway. It's a matter of life and death. My old ma lives there and she's dying. She may not last the week.'

'So?'

'I'll pay double for your ticket.'

'Get lost! I aim to make ten times that when I get to them gold fields.'

'But my mother…'

'Don't sing me that old tune, mister. D'you think I was born yesterday? Go try some other sucker.'

And he pushed Jed back into the crowd knocking him off balance. He couldn't fall because of the number of bodies surrounding him. The other travellers, glad of any diversion to relieve the tedium of waiting on a cold dockside, prodded and pummelled Jed back along the dockside and more than once he thought he was about to land up in the water. The crowd eventually spat him out by some crates at the far end of the dock, on which several other men were seated. As Jed sat down a powerful smell of unwashed clothing and alcohol wafted around him. His nose told him it came from the man sitting next to him who was happily pouring the contents of a whiskey bottle down his throat with gasps of great satisfaction.

'You sailing today?' asked Jed.

The man nodded in response and licked his lips. 'Aaah! Yes. On *The Queen*. God bless her.'

'Didn't you ought to be on board?

'Plenty o' time. Won't go without me.' He took another swig from the bottle. 'I got a ticket.'

'You have?'

The man nodded again and offered Jed the bottle.

Jed shook his head. 'No thanks. What did you pay for it?'

'The whiskey? Hell, I didn't pay for it. I stole it.' The man chuckled happily and upended the bottle yet again.

'No, your ticket. What did you pay for your ticket?'

'One thousand dollars.' And he waved the piece of paper under Jed's nose. 'Can you believe that? My life's savin's.'

'Listen up, mister. I'll give you eleven hundred for that ticket, and my horse. You can sell my horse, and the saddle.' He drew a piece of paper from his pocket and scribbled a few words on it. 'Here's a note that says it's yours to sell, and if you do, you'll have more than enough for another ticket and for equipment too. What d'you say?'

The offer, and its implications, took a long time to sink into the man's whiskey-addled brain. Then, as it began to make sense his mouth, a thin slit in an ugly face, twisted into a cautious smile. 'Let's see your money first.'

Jed took a fold of bills out of his inside pocket.

The man's rheumy eyes lit up when he saw so much cash. 'Count it,' he said.

Jed carefully counted the notes into the man's outstretched hand. 'Twenty – forty - sixty - one hundred - two hundred - eleven hundred dollars.'

'It's a deal.'

They shook on it. Ten minutes later the gangplank was up and *The Queen* steamed out of Seattle with Jed Hansen and hundreds of hopeful miners on board. Jed leaned on the rails watching the docks merge into the mist. It had been too easy cheating that old soak. By sleight of hand, something he was real practised at from the shell game, he had actually only paid five hundred dollars for the steamer ticket. But he salved his conscience by telling himself that the old man had got a good horse and a mighty fine saddle.

As things were to turn out Jed soon began to regret paying even $500 for the ticket. Once they got out to sea it was bitterly cold and there was nowhere he, or anybody else, could escape from the cutting wind. The sea out of Seattle and up to the Gulf of Alaska was wild and rough. *The Queen*, big as she was, was flung from wave to wave like a rowboat, sometimes plunging several stomach-churning feet before re-surfacing only to sink back again. Jed was less than two hours into his voyage before he began to wish he had never come. The nausea surging through his body was intense. The deck heaved and dipped so much he could not stand without being sick. He tried to find somewhere to sit down, a dark space he could crawl into, but the ship was so overloaded there was nowhere private. The decks were strewn with the crouched bodies of other men being violently sick. Jed kicked them aside as he staggered to the side of the boat where he spent the next few hours, leaning over the rails, retching and vomiting and he was not alone.

He spent the next three days in a state of delirium and had never, in all his life, felt so wretched. Nobody took any notice of his suffering because the majority of passengers were in the same plight. He did not wash during those three days, he did not eat and he did care about anything - least of all if he lived or died. But on the third day his stomach, having expelled every last particle of food and fluid, gave up the struggle and settled down. Jed was able to find shelter under a stairway, where a kindly soul lent him a blanket, and gradually he began to feel better. By the fourth day he was able to eat and by the fifth he had found his sea legs.

He got into conversation with a well-dressed man, who came from Montana. 'My name's McKenzie,' he said. 'You've had a rough passage, friend. How are you feeling?'

'Fine, ' said Jed. 'I'll get over it.'

'Good. Let's hope we make it in one piece,' said McKenzie. 'Get a storm out here and…well, ships have gone down- all hands lost - there's no chance of survival in these waters.'

'Is that so? Well, I ain't never been on a boat before and it's not an experience I care to repeat. I shall be more than happy to be on dry land again.'

'Amen to that,' said McKenzie. 'A friend of mine was in Skagway last year and he said you need to have your wits about you. Watch out for pickpockets. You can lose your wallet within seconds of landing. Gangs of no-good villains hang around on the docks just waiting for us newcomers. He said life's cheap and people have gotten killed for their gold or for simply for getting in the way. His actual words were, 'the whole place is lawless scab on the face of humanity, populated with the dregs of the earth and should be avoided at all costs.'

Jed could not resist asking, 'If that's the case what are you doing on this ship?'

'The answer is simple, my friend. Gold and the chance to make a fortune.'

ELEVEN

It was June when *The Queen* steamed into Skagway. The snows, that had prevented any passage through the long, dark winter, had gone and the sky was clear and bright. Once Inuit territory, Skagway had begun as a small village at the base of the Chilkoot Pass, the notorious thirty-two miles and an almost vertical climb to the Klondike gold fields. Horses often lost their footing and fell backwards, taking their rider with them as they tumbled to their death. Some poor animals broke their legs in the rocky crevices and others, overloaded with provisions and equipment, sank into the bogs. Dead or alive, they were all left behind which gave rise to the pass's other name - Dead Horse Trail.

When Jed arrived, the dockside was heaving with humanity. Men unloading supplies from the ship, passengers waiting to get on and a number of unsavoury-looking individuals doing nothing in particular. Jed guessed these must be the gangs his erstwhile travelling companion had warned him about.

The excitement was almost tangible as the boat's passengers disembarked, running and stumbling down the gangplank, eager to be on dry land again. Jed was one of the last to leave the ship and watched with interest as the new arrivals were quickly surrounded by, and absorbed into the throng of hustling bodies. A fight broke out between two men on the quayside. Others joined in and in the scuffle Jed witnessed several wallets being lifted and pockets picked with consummate ease.

Once on the dockside and surrounded by jostling bodies, Jed was acutely aware of nimble fingers searching his own pockets. But he was satisfied they weren't going to find anything. Before leaving Bolterstown he'd had the foresight to conceal most of his money inside his jacket lining and what was left over went, as usual, into his boots.

'Got somewhere to stay, mister?'

Jed was squashed between two burly men who smelled far from sweet. Both had long, greasy hair and beards and their dark hats were pulled well down on their heads leaving little to be seen of their faces.

'Nope!' said Jed. 'Not yet.'

'Go along to Jeff's Place. It's the best saloon in town. If you want a job Jeff'll see you right - and tell him Chuck Ramsay sent you.' He inclined his head towards Jed and his breath was as strong and sour as a jar of year-old pickles. 'But if you want a woman – you come to me. He elbowed Jed in the ribs. 'We got plenty who are willing here. A town full of lonely men far from home what do they want? Womanly comforts and gold. '

'You looking for gold mister?' said his companion, a large, overweight, man with heavy brows and a long, curly beard that could have stuffed a mattress.

'Not exactly,' said Jed. 'But I appreciate your concern, gentlemen.'

'If'n you need anything you come to us, right?' said Ramsay.

Jed recognised it was more of a warning that an act of kindness and had every intention of steering clear of both Ramsay and McGurk. He walked on into Skagway itself which, to his surprise, was not the shanty-town he had expected. Substantial buildings lined the main street, provision merchants of all kinds, clothing stores, gun shops a telegraph office, even a Merchants' Exchange as well as several saloons and gambling halls. The sidewalks were overflowing; the busy street was a heady mix of people, carts, buggies and horses going in all directions and noise. A great deal of noise.

The saloon, recommended by Chuck Ramsay was one of the larger buildings quite close to the docks. Crudely painted in bright red. As Jed stepped up on the sidewalk the doors of Jeff's Place flew open and an old man was thrown out. Jed side-stepped nimbly as the old timer landed heavily. He rolled over and lay on his back for a few seconds looking up at Jed.

'You one o' them?' he said.

'No, sir. Here, let me give you a hand.' Jed helped him up. The old man was thin but Jed could feel the well-developed muscles in his arms.

'Thank you kindly, mister. Jest need to get my breath back.' He brushed down his threadbare jacket, which Jed noted was covered in a light sprinkling of gold dust, picked up his battered and old-fashioned high-crowned hat and rammed it firmly on his head. 'Don't trust anyone in there, boy.' He indicated the saloon. 'They didn't get nuthin' from me and they won't, no sir. Not from old Bill.' He stepped closer to Jed and whispered, 'They don't how much I've got, see, and I ain't about to tell 'em.'

He staggered off, his high hat bobbing along, above the shoulders of the crowd and was soon out of sight. Once inside the saloon, Jed thought no more about him other than he'd probably had too much to drink.

Inside the atmosphere was electric. There were several card games in progress, the players swearing and cursing and jumping up to accuse the other of cheating. Guns were drawn and fights were erupting in every corner while the women screamed encouragement. On stage the dancing girls stamped, shrieked and high-kicked to a small band of musicians trying to make themselves heard above the din. Jed had only just taken a pace inside when somebody grasped his arm. It was a mean looking individual with bad teeth and stubble, who looked as if he hadn't washed in days and by the sour aroma wafting around him, hadn't changed his clothes either.

'Hang up you gunbelt, mister.'

Jed eyed the double-rig worn by the man himself. 'Excuse me?'

'Rules of the house. No guns allowed.'

A quick look round assured Jed that nobody else was wearing guns and there was a full row pegs on the wall so, reluctantly, he removed his rig and hung it up with the others. He had two glasses of red-eye at the bar then collected his guns and left. He didn't ask for Jeff. It hadn't taken him more than a minute or two to size this place up, and his gut instinct told him that it was as crooked as a pig's tail. Out in the busy street he asked the first passer-by where he could get a good clean room for the night.

'Ma Pullen's. Right at the end of the street. It's a pie-shop, and real good too, but she lets out the rooms above.'

On his way through town something oddly familiar caught his attention. It was the tall hat worn by the old man that had been thrown out of the saloon. He was standing in the road talking to a man Jed also recognized – Sam McGurk. Jed, his suspicions aroused, stopped outside one of the stores and pretended to be studying the goods on display.

'How's the claim making out, Bill?' That was McGurk and he sounded friendly enough.

'It's good. I'm doing OK, thanks.'

'I sure hope you've got your poke somewhere safe, Bill. There's folk round here would rob their own grandmother for a speck of gold dust.'

Jed heard old Bill's wheezy laugh followed by, 'I got it safe all right. It's in my money belt.' Jed turned round just in time to see the old man patting his stomach. 'Ain't nobody gonna get that off me without a struggle.'

'Well done, old timer.'

At that point Jed looked round to see McGurk slapping the old man on the back and at the same time signalling with his free hand to somebody on the other side of the street. It was Ramsay. The old man shuffled off but had not gone above ten paces when two men accosted him. Ramsay knocked him to the ground while McGurk pulled up his shirt and stole his money belt. It was clearly a well-rehearsed tactic to relieve prospectors and miners of their gold. Nobody attempted to go after the daylight robbers but several folk were helping old Bill, so Jed left them to it. He could see the two villains melting away into the crowd and set off after them, with little patience for those who got in his way, until somebody caught hold of his collar from behind and jerked him to a halt. 'You're in a real hurry mister!'

'What the hell?' cried Jed.

He spun round to face McGurk. 'You ain't much good at tailing folk, are you, greenhorn?'

'Who says I was tailing anybody? I was just anxious to find me a bed.'

The man laughed. It was an ugly laugh but then he was an ugly man.

'If you want a bed, mister, you want to go right along to the end of town where all the cribs are. Plenty of beds there, and plenty of hookers to fill 'em. '

'It wasn't that kind of bed.'

Jed was walking away when McGurk reached for his arm and stopped him. 'I ain't finished yet. You were listening in on my conversation with that old man and I don't like that. Being spied on ain't nice! I don't know what you think you're up to but, while you're here, you just better pull your ears in, OK? And I don't tell nobody twice.' He thrust Jed aside and swaggered off into the crowd.

Jed knew there was something bad going on here and the sooner he finished his business in Skagway the better. But first things first. He had to find Ma Pullen's crisp and comfortable bed.

TWELVE

The following morning, after a good night's rest and one of Ma Pullen's tasty beef pies for breakfast, Jed went out to have a look at this notorious town. Somewhere round here Soapy Smith hung out. Although Jed had replaced his lost payroll many times over with his own swindles, being so dumb as to lose all that hard-earned money still rankled.

The streets were just as busy as the day before. Some folk were clearly regular citizens of Skagway; people who had made a home here and were trying to make a living but the majority were miners or prospectors. They flooded into Skagway day after day, to buy provisions and equipment for their journey up to the Klondike. The men, and it was nearly all men, were far from home and vulnerable and it was an ideal environment for thieves, cheats and pickpockets. Since there was nowhere else to buy such goods it also meant the opportunist storekeepers, provision merchants, bankers and horse-traders of Skagway were able to charge any sum they liked for their goods and services. It crossed Jed's mind that he could earn a mean buck here for himself. Jed continued his thoughtful progress along the main street until he got to Clancy's Bar. Two men were sitting outside on a bench enjoying a chew of tobacco and appeared to be doing nothing more than watching the world go by. On the other hand, he cautioned himself, they could be lookouts working for McGurk or some other hustler. Both wore double rigs and were as ugly as sin, one more than the other with a jagged scar on his cheek. They looked like hard men and they looked dangerous. Jed wasn't going to take any chances on his first day in town so he touched the brim of his hat.

'G'morning, gentlemen. Fine day.'

The men looked him up and down and nodded. 'Jest arrived?' asked one, spitting his wad into the road.

'Yep. Yesterday, on *The Queen*.'

'Heading for the Klondike?'

'Nope. Stopping here for a while.'

The conversation was brought to a halt by a noisy disturbance on the other side of the street. There were maybe ten or fifteen men marching down the street and more were joining as they went along.

'What's that all about?' asked Jed.

The two men shrugged but made no attempt to move. 'Always somethin' going on,' said one.

Then they were cries of '*String him up!*' and Jed saw a rope being flung over a tree. The crowd jeered and whooped as they pressed forward. A man with his hands tied behind his back, and loudly proclaiming his innocence, was lifted onto the back of a cart and a noose placed around his neck.

'It's a lynching!' said Jed. 'Didn't think this sort thing went on anymore.'

'It's his own fault,' said one of the two men behind him, 'He got folk's dander up. Murdered two men in cold blood. Men with wives and families.'

'That's as maybe,' said Jed, his eyes still drawn to the baying lynch mob 'but don't he get a trial?' Flashbacks reminded Jed of the men he had killed, always he protested in self-defence, although he knew there were some who might argue to contrary.

'He don't need no trial,' said a new voice, a rich velvet voice with a strong Southern States drawl. 'Most folks would agree with that 'cepting maybe those pain-in-the-ass vigilantes. Speak of the devil, boys, here comes the leader himself. Mr Frank Reid who's got his fingers in every darned pie.'

A well-dressed man, in his mid thirties or so, came running down the road and thrust himself into the crowd just as the lynching gang was about to perform the final act.

'Cut that man down!' he yelled. 'You can't do this!'

But they wanted blood and his plea went unheard. Frank then took out his gun and fired into the air. 'Cut him down!' he repeated, now that he had their attention. 'Lynching's unlawful and you know it!'

His remarks were greeted with hoots of derision. Somebody shouted out. 'What law? He's murdered two men. He deserves to die!'

'I don't care what he's done or supposed to have done,' cried Frank. 'Whoever he is, he deserves a fair trial. Now cut him down.'

'He'll only go and kill someone else!' shrilled a female voice. 'We can't afford to take that risk.'

The mob noisily agreed and Frank was obliged to fire again. 'Cut him down and I'll see he's safe until he goes to trial. Then, if he's guilty he deserves all the punishment he gets.'

It seemed that some agreed that there should be a trial while others complained because they were denied the spectacle of a hanging. It looked to Jed as if most of them still wanted a lynching but Frank's reasoned persistence won the day.

'So what are you goin' to do with him?' said the self-appointed hangman as he reluctantly handed his victim over.

'I'm going to take him to the jailhouse, where he belongs, and you ...' he turned to address the now silent crowd, ' . . . can all go about your business or go home.'

Frank hustled his prisoner over to the sidewalk to where Jed, and his fellow onlookers, was standing.

'Out of my way,' said Frank, 'I want to get this man under lock and key as quickly as possible.'

Then the rich velvet voice said, 'Leave it Reid. I'm the law around here. You hand him over to me.'

Jed turned round expecting to see a Town Sheriff or a Marshal but instead found himself staring into the handsome, bearded face on his wanted poster – the face of Soapy Smith.

THIRTEEN

'Hand him over?' said Frank, 'Why should I? You're no lawman. I'll put him away where he belongs till a marshal gets here.'

Smith did not move but with an unsettling and sardonic smile on his face stood directly in Frank's way preventing him from making progress. They stood head to head for some time as the bustle of Skagway life continued around them. Jed could see the open hostility between the two men and had a gut feeling that Reid was a fellow protagonist where Smith was concerned and any enemy of Smith's was a friend of his.

'I'll help you, Mr Reid,' he said, taking the prisoners' other arm. 'Where's the jailhouse?'

'You ain't bin here long have you, mister,' sneered the man with the scar on his face.

'Long enough,' said Jed, 'to know there's a helluva lot of thievin' going on and not much respect for the law or for people's belongings.'

'You're asking for trouble, mister,' said the man Frank had rescued from the lynch mob. 'And don't think I ain't grateful to you for savin' my neck, but if you want to save yours then hand me over, like he says.'

'You hear that, Reid?' said Smith. 'You'd be wise to take his advice.' The charismatic smile had now disappeared. 'And don't cross me again, newcomer.' This was directed at Jed. 'I'm a man who bears grudges. Just be warned.'

'OK' said Frank. 'You can take him, Smith, but I'll be along to the jail later to make sure he's there and I'm telling you I intend to see that man gets a fair trial.'

'You, mister busybody Reid,' said Smith, 'are beginning to get right under my skin. Just keep out of my way, you hear me, and you'll probably live. Now, let's move on. I don't like arguin' in the street. It ain't my style.'

When Smith and his men had gone Frank turned to Jed and said, 'Allow me to shake your hand, sir. I appreciate your support. There are not many in this town who would stand up to that man. My name is Frank

Reid, as you may have gathered and I am the town architect and leader of the local vigilantes.'

'Jed Hansen. Pleased to meet you.'

'Let me buy you a drink, Mr Hansen.' And as they walked along, 'I take it you don't think much of this place.'

'Well, it don't seem too friendly.'

'I didn't mean the people,' said Frank, 'or that rogue Smith, I meant what do think of the streets, the roads, the layout? We have proper drainage here, you know.'

'It's mighty fine. I was expecting a whole heap of mud and a few shanties.'

'And so it was, my friend. When I got here last year that's exactly what it was. I laid this town out. I put a lot of thought and money into it. I am a civil engineer by profession, you see, and I could see that with the new gold strikes in the Klondike, this little place had great potential. Everybody has to come here to get to the Chilkoot Pass. There's no other way to them gold fields.'

'You seem to have made a good job of it, Mr Reid.'

'Call me Frank. Yes, outwardly, that's so, but that man Smith is the bug in my underwear! Since he and his no-good gang of cut throats turned up, things have been real bad. He came here with five men, *five*, and now has upwards of thirty in his pay – murderers and thieves the lot of them. And any number of hangers-on, fraudsters and Bunco men all running their own fraudulent games. The few honest citizens of this town don't stand a chance anymore.'

'And the law? Don't that count?'

'My friend, we are a thousand miles from any kind of real law. That rogue Smith makes his own laws. He can do what he likes - and he mostly does.'

The fact that Soapy Smith was running this town was bad news for Jed. Getting the upper hand and taking any kind of revenge was going to be a lot harder than he first thought. He and Frank had walked a good way by now and Jed discovered that Skagway was a pretty big town.

'Must be twenty thousand people or more, live here now,' said Frank proudly. They had walked two or three blocks and into another street when he stopped outside a handsome, blue-painted saloon. 'This here's Annie's Parlour. One of the best in town *and* one of the few businesses not owned by Smith.'

The atmosphere inside could not have been more of a contrast to Jeff's Place. There were silk drapes on the walls, paintings, and four pink chandeliers that cast a warm glow over the tables and the plush, velvet sofas. Inside Frank and Jed were greeted by a smiling, blue-eyed blonde in a green satin dress with an upward thrusting bodice that displayed her fulsome figure to perfection.

'Would you gentleman like a table, or would you prefer to drink at the bar?'

She had a soft voice and beautiful teeth. Jed was instantly smitten. He hadn't given any thought to women for a long while. His sickness on the boat had erased all such desires but now, they came flooding back.

'A table,' said Frank, briskly. 'Somewhere private, if you please.'

The vision, who told them her name was Eleanor, 'Nelly to my intimates,' showed them to a table under a balcony. Leaning forwards provocatively, allowing Jed and Frank every opportunity to survey her substantial charms, she said, 'Whiskey gentlemen? Annie supplies only the best. Can I get you a bottle?'

'Sure can,' said Jed, bestowing on Nelly one of his most seductive smiles. 'And how about yourself?'

'Later,' interrupted Frank. 'Time for all that later. Thank you, Nelly.' Then to Jed, 'What's your business here, Mr Hansen, if you don't mind me asking? Are you planning to do some prospecting? There's not much else going to do here and I don't take you for a shopkeeper.'

Jed smiled. 'It's a long story but the fact is, It's a personal matter between me and Soapy Smith. I've been trailing him for some time.'

'Well, there's plenty of folk here hold grudges against that man. And, by the way, he's not known as Soapy anymore. He calls himself by his real name, Jefferson Smith. When he got here he made out he was some kind of honest citizen – putting up money for this and that, contributing to good causes and ingratiating himself with the townsfolk. Oh yes, he did a good job. He fooled everybody - excepting me and a few others. In fact that man is behind every crooked operation going on here, but does he ever soils his own hands? No, sir! And it's hard to pin anything on him because he let's others do the dirty work for him.'

'Where does he hang out?'

'He runs all his business from the back of Jeff's Place.'

'So that's *his*, is it?' Jed recalled the old miner being thrown out and callously robbed.

'He owns darned near everything here. Jeff's Place, Clancy's Bar, The Golden Nugget, most of the whorehouses, he's got those girls working for him too...the Merchant's Exchange even the Telegraph Office. As for the Gambling Halls, well you'd need to be drunk or loco, or both to think you could win anything in there. And the telegraphs don't go nowhere. He makes you pay to send and collect. Then invents his own replies usually in the form of requests for money so he gets two bites of the cherry.'

'But surely folk would know that. Once bitten...'

'Oh too right, but there's new folks coming through Skagway all the time. Hundreds of them and most as green as grass.'

Nelly returned with a dazzling smile, the whiskey and two glasses. Frank was searching his pockets for cash.

'No, I'll pay for this,' said Jed, as he slipped a ten-dollar bill between Nelly's creamy breasts. 'My pleasure.'

'Why thank you kindly,' she said, her sparkling eyes devouring Jed as the tip of her tongue outlined her rose-pink lips.

'What we need,' said Frank, who did not even look up, 'is more folk like yourself. Willing to stand up for what's right. What d'you say?'

'About what?' said Jed, dragging his thoughts away from the delectable Nelly.

'About joining the vigilantes.'

'Oh, I don't think so.'

'Now, don't be too hasty. Hear me out. There's a lot of honest folk here who want rid of Smith. Who want their town back, who want law and order restored.'

'Didn't I see someone wearing a sheriff's badge?'

'Oh yeah, but he ain't no real lawman. He's in Smith's pay too. He spent time in the penitentiary for killing someone. We had a marshal here for a while but he was shot by one of Smith's men. Well, you can't shoot a lawman and get away with it so that's when we formed the vigilantes. Called ourselves the Committee of 101, because one hundred and one signed up, and we tried to get the murderer hung. But as soon as Smith found out his men started rioting and looting all over town. They broke into the warehouses, robbed folk in the streets, our homes and families were threatened – and they were no idle threats.'

'I admire what you're doing,' said Jed, 'but I'm not your man.'

'You've got guts,' said Frank. 'And you're not afraid of facing up to those bullies. Seems to me you're exactly the man. The way I see it is, if we all work together we can do something. But individually...' He shook his head. '...we've got no chance.'

While Frank had been talking Jed had been quietly consuming most of the whiskey and was now feeling ready for some action. Nelly was serving just a couple of tables away. An over-amorous customer had her on his lap and was drooling down the front of her dress. Jed caught her eye and signalled for her to come over. She smiled and nodded and after kissing the man on his balding head, extricated herself with dignity from his drunken embrace. Frank was still going on about his committee and what needed to be done when Jed suddenly stood up.

'That all sounds good, Frank.'

'Oh,' Frank looked surprised. 'You're going? But you'll think about what I said?'

'Sure I will.'

Nelly's fragrant body was so close, and smelled so sweet, that Jed could hardly restrain himself from running up the stairs.

'Which room?' he asked, when they got to the top.

'Number seven...the road to heaven.'

Jed could not get there quick enough.

FOURTEEN

The following day, when Jed went into town, he sensed something was going on. He overheard comments such as, 'We ain't safe in our beds anymore,' and 'We should'a hanged him when we had the chance.'

He all but collided with a furious Frank Reid. ' He's done it again.'

'Who's done what?'

'That man you rescued from the hanging. He's escaped from jail.'

'How'd he manage that?'

'Not on his own, that's for sure. I think Jeff Smith is behind this. Some of his men shot the guard and got that murdering swine out. He's on a boat by now. I'm dammed sure of it. I tell you, Jed, the sooner we get a marshal and some law and order here the better. He was probably one of Smith's men anyway.'

'But Smith didn't seem too concerned when he was about to be hung.'

'No. I daresay he thought he deserved it – couldn't have cared less but as soon as I got my hands on him, tried to do the decent thing, well, that was a different matter. It was a chance to get one over on me.'

They were only a few paces away from Annie's Parlour and Jed, anxious to see Nelly again, suggested they go there for a drink and maybe talk things over.

'This place seems to be well patronised,' said Jed. 'A little goldmine in Skagway, wouldn't you say?'

'Well, there's a big shortage of women here, as you might have noticed,' said Frank. 'There's always the hookers and fallen doves, plenty of those, but this place has class and it's run by classy lady, too.'

There were no unoccupied tables so Jed and Frank stood at the bar.

'You know what I think this town needs,' said Frank. 'A good dose of religion.'

Jed laughed. 'How's that gonna help?'

'There's nothing here but greed and vice. Folk need to be shown the straight and narrow.'

Jed, thinking of his parents' strong beliefs and Spartan life-style, wasn't so sure that would work in Skagway. He'd just met the lovely Nelly and didn't want no straight and narrow right now.

'I'm going to put it to the committee,' said Frank, downing his drink. 'We're meeting at 2 o'clock today in the town hall. You're welcome to come, Jed.'

When Frank left, the two men standing next to him also drank up and left and Jed was alone at the bar. There were several comely women in Annie's Parlour for Jed to savour but, disappointingly, Nelly was not one of them. He ordered another drink. He wondered if Nelly was upstairs, maybe with a client. There was a large sofa by the sweeping staircase so Jed took his drink and sat over there. He reckoned that if she was upstairs, when she came down she'd be sure to see him.

He did not have to wait long. The rustle of satin told him that somebody was coming, maybe Nelly, maybe not. He did not look up but feigned in-difference, finishing off his drink. The rustling ceased as a woman stood directly in front of him. Jed's eyes travelled up from the hem of the red satin dress, under which was a neat little satin shoe, to the narrow waist, the smooth, pale arms and the lacy bodice which barely covered her bosom.

'Weren't you in here, yesterday, Jed Hansen?'

Jed gasped as he stared at the familiar face framed by tumbling red curls. 'Mary-Anne!' He stood up and looked her up and down apprecia-tively taking in every last detail of her expensive dress and fancy hair-do. 'Mary-Anne! Am I glad to see you and looking as tasty as ever.'

Mary-Anne ignored Jed's outstretched arms and sat down on the sofa. 'Sit down, Jed.' She patted the plush cushions. 'So what have you been doing all this while.'

'I didn't forget you. I came to look for you as soon as I could.'

'I waited a whole day and a night when you didn't show, I figured somethin' musta happened to you and I'd best look out for myself.'

'Somethin' did happen. I was injured real bad,' said Jed. 'The posse was right behind me when I went off the track … right down the other side of the mountain.' He paused. 'It was awhile before I was well enough to come lookin'.' He deliberately chose not to mention Betsy Catchpole.

She and Toomey were all in the past and it wouldn't help none to go over all that again. 'Then I found out Smith was operating up this way and here I am. How did you get along, Mary-Anne?'

'I did what I've always done and it pays well. Then I heard about the gold and silver strikes - and here I am too. It suited me just fine. Plenty of men, with plenty of money and not enough women! A ready-made market and I took advantage of it.'

'You're really are somethin', Mary-Anne.'

'I ain't called that anymore. I'm known as Annie here. Mary-Anne's Parlour just didn't sound right somehow. Sort of prissy and more like a prayer house, you know what I mean?'

Jed let this piece of information sink in before he said, 'Are you telling me you own this place?'

'Sure do. Every last stick of it and I make a good profit too. Too good for some folks - Jeff Smith for one. He'd like to buy me out. His men come in here regular but I can usually spot 'em. There were two next to you and Frank Reid at the bar just now. Ears a-flappin' and a'listenin' out for information that they can take back to their boss.'

'Is there somewhere private we can go?' asked Jed. 'To catch up on old times?' He smiled and his eyes twinkled seductively.

'I have a suite upstairs,' said Mary-Anne, 'but I have to tell you I ain't for sale no more. I am a business woman now but if you want entertainment I can recommend my girls. They're all clean and hand picked.'

Jed thought of all the women he had been with over the years and, most recently, the delectable Nelly but not one had had the same effect on him as Mary-Anne; soft and beautiful on the outside but tough as nails within. She had grit, she had guts and she had done well for herself. Better than he had in many ways.

'I'd be right happy, ma-am to be entertained with a humble cup of coffee so long as I could have the additional pleasure of your company.'

Mary-Anne laughed. 'You always did have a way with words, Jed Hansen. Come on up.'

Jed didn't believe for one minute that the fiery Mary-Anne could or would resist him once they were alone. Her private suite was sumptuous in the extreme, thick, rich carpets, elegant furniture and discreet lighting.

And she served his coffee on a silver tray.

'I got to hand it to you Mary-Anne,' said Jed, 'you sure made something of yourself.'

'And it ain't been easy. I worked hard for this place and I ain't givin' it up without a fight. Sit down. Make yourself at home.'

Jed chose a large and very comfortable button-backed sofa and Mary-Anne sat beside him.

'Round here there's plenty that would like a share in my business. Some of 'em by offering to marry me and some, like Jeff Smith, by making life difficult so's I'd want to sell out.'

'How's he doing that?'

'Hell, *he* don't do nothing except make eyes at me, but his men do. I've been burgled more than once, my girls have been bad-mouthed around town which ain't good for trade. He's even threatened to kill me.'

'Would it help if I hung around?' said Jed. 'I could provide protection.'

'That's right kind of you, Jed, but I can manage. If I need extra help I'll ask for it.'

Jed emptied his cup in one swig then sat back and watched Mary-Anne sipping her drink and looking every inch the lady. When she put the cup back on the tray Jed put his arm around her waist and drew her towards him. He could feel her corseted breasts pressing against his chest. He wanted this woman and he wanted her now. His mouth closed over hers and her lips responded to his kiss as he fumbled with the buttons at the back of her bodice.

'No, Jed no.' Mary-Anne suddenly pulled back and stood up. 'Like I said, I'm not for sale anymore.'

'Hell! When did I ever pay you -'cepting that first time?' Jed, aroused and angry, stood up and pulled Mary-Anne round to face him. 'Why so coy all of a sudden? What's this all about?'

'Things have changed. This is *my* place and *I'm* in control now. I can chose what I do and when I do it.'

'And who you do it with.'

Mary-Anne gently detached herself from Jed's hold. 'Well, now we've got that straight, maybe we could have something to eat.'

'Thank you, no!' said Jed. 'I've kinda lost my appetite.'

FIFTEEN

Jed was awoken the following morning by the sounds of Ma Pullen banging on his door saying he'd got a visitor downstairs.

'A visitor? At this hour?' He peered squint-eyed out of the window. It was barely sun-up.

'It's that Mr Reid and he's mighty fired up about somethin'.'

Jed flung a blanket round his shoulders and followed her downstairs. He found Frank pacing up and down in the shop. When he saw Jed he waved the local paper in the air and then smacked it down on the counter.

'Now d'you see what I mean? Read that!' He was pointing to an article on the front page of *The Klondike Nugget* about a Skagway woman who was murdered in her bed. 'That's Mrs Henderson, wife of one of our town officials and a nicer woman you couldn't wish to meet. Murdered! Robbed and murdered in her own home and d'you know who did it? Smith's gang, that's who. Jed we desperately need somebody like you to help us, somebody who's not easily scared. What d'you say?'

'Don't ask me no more, Frank. I ain't cut out to be a vigilante or any kind of law enforcer. Truth to tell I'm wanted by the law myself. I've cheated and killed men without thinking twice. I ain't your man.'

'Hell, there's been plenty of lawmen who started out as outlaws or gunslingers. I don't pay no mind to that. I've been in trouble myself but we've got to think of something to prevent Smith's stranglehold on this town. And we've got to act quickly. Let me know if you change your mind.'

Frank went out slamming the shop door which made the tin bell over the top rattle furiously bringing Ma Pullen rushing in from her kitchen.

'Somebody else come in?'

'No, Ma. Mr Reid just left.'

'How I'm supposed to get today's pies ready with all this comin' and going'? Lock that shop door, Mr Hansen. I don't want no more interruptions.'

Ma Pullen returned to her kitchen and Jed to his bed. No need to be up this early. The way he saw it Frank wanted Smith out of Skagway immediately, today, tomorrow, yesterday even, but that wasn't going to happen. Jefferson Smith had got this town, and its officials, in his back pocket and it was unlikely to change until the real law put in an appearance. Frank had recently received word that a deputy marshal might be coming soon but, for now, Jed was content for Smith to stay right where he was - under his nose.

He woke up in the morning with a pain in his stomach and tried to remember what he'd eaten last night. After he'd left Mary-Anne he was feeling pretty low so he visited a few saloons, quite a few, to raise his spirits. And it worked. He smiled as he remembered that pretty little dark-haired vixen who took him back to her crib but after that it was kind of hazy. His gut was screaming again and he doubled up, clutching his belly. It wasn't the beer or the whiskey…that had never had this sort of effect on him. Could it be Ma's pies? He'd had a glut of them lately but Ma Pullen had a reputation to uphold – a good one that she prized above all else. He staggered downstairs feeling dizzy and slightly nauseous.

The door to the back of the shop had a glass panel in it and he could see Ma busily selling to a shop full of customers. He knew she wouldn't like being taken away from her trade but it didn't stop him knocking.

'What is it?' said Ma, fifteen minutes later.

'Where's the nearest Doc, Ma. I ain't well.' Jed slumped to the floor in agony.

'Lord have mercy. You ain't going nowhere's like that, young man. Jest let me shut the shop and I'll get you up to bed. Then I'll fetch the Doc.'

'No, Ma. Fetch the Doc first. I'll manage.'

A few minutes later, Doctor McKinnock called. He took one look at Jed and said, 'Ah yes. I know what this is. I'll give you something that will ease the pain.' He was a neatly dressed man more like a parson than a doctor, in a black frock coat, wing collar and bow tie. 'You're Jed Hansen, right?' Jed nodded. 'I thought I recognized you. You were the one who stopped that man from being lynched.'

Jed was unsure whether the Doc approved or disapproved of his action. He had a way of speaking that lacked any kind of emotion. McKinnock took a medicine bottle out of his bag and poured a few drops into the glass of water by Jed's bed. 'Drink this, Mr Hansen, and you will feel much better.'

Afterwards he said he remembered drinking the medicine but nothing else. He must have fallen asleep again because when he woke up it was late afternoon. The pain had gone but so had his wallet and the extra cash hidden in his boots.

Ma Pullen offered her commiseration. 'I'm so sorry Mr Hansen. I ain't never called on that man before. He just happened to be passing when I ran out of the shop in a panic and he said he was a doctor.'

How convenient thought Jed, and last night with the hooker? What had she given him? He knew he'd been well and truly set up and he knew who was behind it.

SIXTEEN

The following day, and fully recovered, Jed called on Frank and told him what had happened.

'Didn't I warn you?' said Frank. 'This town is full of crooks and confidence tricksters. You don't trust anybody. That man was no more a medical man than you or I. He's in Smith's pay and it isn't the first time he's pulled a trick like that. He's robbed men and women alike in this town - especially the women. He looks and acts the part, gets their confidence, then drugs them and steals whatever's to hand.'

'Well, he sure cleaned me out.'

'I'm not a rich man, Jed, but...' Frank took out his wallet and handed Jed fifty dollars. 'Pay me back when you can.'

Jed was grateful for Frank's kindness but unless he could get work there was no way he could pay him back. So, a couple of days later he decided to try his luck in one of the many Skagway gambling halls. He had not been in The Silver Dollar before and he knew it was more than likely that all the games were fixed, but he reckoned he stood as good a chance as anyone of making a few bucks with the cards. He was a skilled poker player and well-versed in sleight of hand and as long as nobody challenged him, what harm did it do? Two hours later Jed came out $200 better off than he went in and there had been no need to resort to guns or violence. All in all he considered it a good day's work.

Apart from paying back the fifty dollars Jed saw very little of Frank over the next two weeks. Any spare time Frank had he dedicated to the work of the vigilantes. Two more weeks passed and Jed was no nearer thinking of a way to outsmart Smith and for that matter neither was Frank. He had, true to his word, and in spite of a lack of funds, got a preacher to come to Skagway. A retired parson, living in Seattle, who was undaunted by Skagway's bad reputation. Parson Glover was a man with a mission, keen to spread the word of the Lord in such lawless, heathen outposts. To the surprise of Frank and his committee, Smith greeted the arrival of the parson with delight. He sent his men out into town with collecting boxes 'For the Preacher.' They went into every house, the saloons, the gambling halls, even the whorehouses and collected the amazing sum of $35,000 which Smith made a big show of handing over, in public, to the stunned and flattered churchman.

'I don't get it,' said Frank to Jed, who both witnessed the presentation. 'He's up to something.'

Sure enough, that night the unsuspecting parson was robbed while he slept.

'I knew it,' raged Frank, the next day. 'I knew he had some mean trick up his sleeve.' Frank had called Jed over to his house. 'We are being made fools of by this man. He's got us all dancing to his tune. Now, I have not been idle all these weeks. The Committee has had these posters made and I want you to help me get them up around town. What do you think of them?'

Jed studied the posters.

ALL OUTLAWS, CROOKS, BUNCO MEN
QUACKS AND CONFIDENCE TRICKSTERS
TO LEAVE TOWN TODAY.
IF NOT THE LAW WILL TAKE ITS COURSE
Signed: The committee of 101, Skagway

'What do you mean by 'the law will take its course?' asked Jed. 'They're ain't no law. That's the problem.'

'I mean we'll have to run them out of town.'

Jed knew how desperate Frank was to be rid of these men but threatening action without the backing of the law was never going to work.

'You realise what that means? They won't go without a fight and it won't be a fair one. Bet your boots.'

'I know that but I'm ready.' Frank was resolute.

Jed was walking down the main street on his way to Annie's Parlour when he saw Smith reading one of the posters. Smith saw Jed and walked towards him.

'Listen Hansen. You can tell your friend Reid, that if he thinks a few greenhorns are gonna scare me by putting up these piddling notices then he's got it wrong. I can take this fight to any length he cares to mention, and if it comes to a shootout - that so called bunch of vigilantes won't stand a snowball's chance in hell against my men. You got that?'

'I got it,' said Jed. 'But I ain't deliverin' it. You got somethin' to say to him, you say it yourself.'

Smith stared at Jed long and hard. Then he said, 'You don't look like an idiot but you sure are acting like one.'

Jed grinned. 'Well, you should know. You got plenty working for you.'

Smith smiled but his eyes were hard. 'You know, you're beginning to irritate me, Hansen, just like your stubborn friend. What exactly is your business here anyway?'

'Whatever it is, it's *my* business.'

'Well, here's a piece of advice you'd do well to take note of. Get it done quick and move on.'

'That's just what I intend to do,' said Jed. 'Good day to you.'

He touched the brim of his hat and sauntered off towards Annie's Parlour. He did not look back but guessed that Smith was watching to see where he went.

He'd seen Mary-Anne most days and was sure she still had feelings for him but for some unknown reason she wasn't giving way to them. She was keeping him at arm's length and he intended to find out why. She always took him upstairs but never for the reason Jed hoped. They had tea, or coffee, sometimes something stronger and they talked - but that was all. But on this particular day Mary-Anne came running down the stairs to meet him. She looked even prettier than usual with her flushed cheeks and Jed's hopes began to rise. She tucked her arm in his and led him upstairs. Once in her sitting room she guided him towards the sumptuous sofa but she sat opposite him in an armchair.

'Jed. We need to talk. Just what are you doing here?'

He smiled. 'Why I'm waiting for you to thaw out, Mary-Anne and come and sit over here.'

'I mean what are you doing in Skagway?'

'What sort of question is that? You know what I'm doing. I'm here because Smith's here. Because he swindled me and I want retribution. If I can't do that I sure as hell want to see him suffer. '

'OK, but I don't hear nothin' about what you're actually gonna do?'

'No. I ain't rightly got it fixed in my head yet. But it's taken me durned near a year to find him. I ain't in no hurry.'

'Well you should be! I saw him talking to you just now and don't tell me he was enquirin' after your health. You've made an enemy of him, Jed, and he's not known for his patience. Hell, does it matter any more? You've taken enough money off folks since to replace that payroll. Now either do somethin' about that chip on your shoulder or fergit it and get on with your life.'

When she finished speaking Mary-Anne bowed her head and Jed could see her pink cheeks redden still further.

'S'funny. Smith just said somethin' similar, only not so pretty-like.'

There was urgency in Mary-Anne's voice when she next spoke. 'I ain't talking pretty. I mean it, Jed. Smith and his gang murder people like they're picking flowers. They're ruthless all of 'em and Smith ain't got no feelings for nobody but himself. I told you how he wants this place and he's threatening me with big trouble if I don't cut him in. And I ain't gonna do that because he don't want no partnership he wants control. Now he's discovered that we're old friends and he's using that to get at me.'

'How come?'

'Holy Moses, Jed! Is your brain so full of Ma Pullen's pies? He knows I care for you! He knows I wouldn't want anything to happen to you! So, your life is the deal breaker. Now do you get it?' Mary-Anne stood up and flounced towards the window where she stood, hands on hips, her back to Jed, who remained seated. 'I've been able to deal with him up to now but you turning up has made things a darned sight harder!' She took a deep breath before she spoke again. 'So, like I said, Jed, you either do somethin' about it or.....'

'I leave town.'

Jed stood up and walked over to Mary-Anne. He put his arms around her waist and said, 'I'm plum crazy about you. You know that don't you? Think I always have been. When I couldn't find you, after we split up, I thought I'd never see you again so I tried to put you out of my mind - but

I missed you, something bad.'

Gently he turned her round to face him. He expected to see moist eyes tears even, but there were none. He told himself he should have known better. Mary-Anne was one tough cookie and visions of the murdered Penfold suddenly flashed through his mind. The only sign of any anxiety was the way the colour on her cheeks travelled down her neck. While admiring her very desirable body he could not help wondering if she still carried that knife.

'So? What's it to be Jed?'

'I want to stay here. I want to be with you. I'd like us...'

'Ain't you heard a word I said. There will be no 'us' Jed Hansen until Smith is out of our lives. One way or another he has to be dealt with and it won't be pretty.'

'He don't scare me, Mary-Anne.'

'But he sure as hell should!' She stamped her foot and broke away from his embrace. 'You just don't see it, do you! I've worked my guts out to make this place a success and I can be just as ruthless as Smith if I need to. Now for myself, I can deal with it but I have feelings for you, Jed, and I don't want to see you hurt.'

'Well, things ain't quite turned out the way I expected,' said Jed. 'And I sure didn't figure on Smith having this town in his back pocket. Seems there's bigger things to worry about than my lost payroll and I sure wouldn't want any harm to come to you Mary-Anne. You mean too much to me.'

Once again his charm won Mary-Anne over - so much so that they ended up in her boudoir – a breathtaking vision of pink lace and purple drapes tied with golden tassels. But Jed barely noticed such things. He only had eyes for Mary-Anne.

SEVENTEEN

The next meeting of the vigilantes was held at Frank's house. Somehow or other Smith found out and while the meeting was in progress Frank's house was raided. Windows were broken, furniture smashed, precious belongings stolen or destroyed and several committee members hurt, including Frank. Smith's message was plain to all. If you want war you can have it.

Frank, who had sustained several blows and cuts to the head, during the attack was being looked after by a neighbour who came in each day to see how he was. When Jed went to visit, Frank was pacing about his front parlour with an outsize bandage around his head.

'I'm fine,' he said in answer to Jed's enquiry. 'It's not serious. Just a few scratches. And I don't need this ridiculous thing.' He pulled off the blood-stained bandage.

'I hear Smith's putting up some money for a 4th of July Parade,' said Jed.

'Yes, that's what I've heard. Yet another chance for him to ingratiate himself with the townsfolk and the newcomers. Poor deluded fools. They'll soon learn.'

On the 4th July Mary-Anne closed Annie's Parlour so that she and her girls could go to the Parade. The town was decked out with bunting and all the inhabitants and miners in high spirits. Smith, who rode at the head of the Parade on a magnificent white charger, had made himself a Grand marshal for the occasion. He wore a purple sash over his suit and as he passed he doffed his hat to left and right.

'I can't stand no more of this,' said Mary-Anne. 'That man makes me want to puke. I'm going back to the Parlour. There's some paperwork I'd like to get done while it's quiet. You girls enjoy yourself."

Jed, meanwhile, had stayed as far away from the Parade as he could. He was enjoying a quiet drink with the elderly owner of a run down old bar who was more than grateful for Jed's custom.

As soon as Mary-Anne put her key in the door of Annie's Parlour she knew something was wrong because it was not locked and she was very particular about locking up. Maybe for once she had been careless but it was unlikely. She pushed the door and let it swing open. Even though the blinds were down it all looked perfectly normal but as soon as she put her foot over the threshold someone grabbed her arm and pulled her inside. She heard the door slam shut behind her.

'Let's have some light, ' said the man holding her. 'I want to have a good look at this little beauty.'

The gaslights went up and Mary-Anne found herself surrounded by a gang of Smith's men, several of whom she recognized and one in particular, that animal Hank Dawson. Try though she did she could not stop that chilling wave of fear from coursing through her veins. Dawson had a penchant for weird and violent sex. He had raped any number of women in the town, prostitutes and virgins alike and Mary-Anne had banned him for life from Annie's Parlour after he tried it on with one of her girls. Now he was looking her over and licking his fat lips like he was already planning something wild and disgusting as a revenge for denying him.

'What's this all about,' she said, trying to remain dignified and keep a note of authority in her voice.

'Nothing' much, Annie, gal,' said Wes Bruton. 'We just felt like a bit of entertainment.'

'We're closed!' said Mary-Anne, defiantly, though her heart was turning somersaults inside her bodice. She knew of Bruton's reputation with women and was seriously worried. Everybody was at the Parade, the bands were playing, the crowds roaring, whatever they did, however much she cried for help, nobody would hear. 'Look. They're ain't nobody here. I'll do a deal with you.'

'What sort of deal?' asked Wes.

'You go quietly, and I'll see you get personal treatment next time you call.'

Wes, and the others, hooted with derisive laughter. 'We know what to expect from your personal treatment, Annie. As soon as you got one of us on our own, we'd sure as hell find ourselves looking down the barrel of that cute derringer you keep tucked away in your pocket.'

He reached under Annie's apron and had a good feel around before he found the gun. With her free hand Mary-Anne slapped him hard across the face.

'Keep your filthy hands off me,' she hissed. 'You're scum. All of you. Get out of here!' Her knee came up and she thrust her heel backward into the man who was holding her. He cursed loudly and let go, moaning and clutching his groin.

'Why you little vixen!' said Wes, seizing Mary-Anne as she made a run for the door. 'But I like a woman with spirit. Makes for a good time. Ain't that right boys?'

'Let me have her,' growled Hank, stumbling forward in his eagerness. 'I'll knock some sense into the bitch.'

'You'll take your turn,' said Wes, 'Billy, Poke, and you Hank, come with me. We're gonna take this hellcat upstairs and while we're busy…the rest of you - trash this place and trash it good.'

Mary-Anne kicked, screamed and swore as she was manhandled up to the stairs and into her bedroom. But she was no match for four brutal, sex-crazed men.

EIGHTEEN

When Jed went round to Annie's Parlour later that afternoon he found the place trashed. The beautiful drapes ripped, the crystal chandelier shot to a million pieces and the velvet furniture slashed and torn. After the initial shock Jed's first thoughts were for Mary-Anne. He ran up the stairs two and three at a time. Her sitting room was as bad, if not worse, than downstairs. Sick at heart for what he might find he flung open the door to the boudoir. Mary-Anne lay on the bed stark naked and bleeding.

'Mary-Anne,' Jed fell on his knees beside the bed. 'Mary-Anne.' He held her hand. 'Who did this to you?' He drew the satin sheets over her. 'Mary-Anne? Open your eyes. Say somethin'. Jest let me know you're in there.'

For several mind-numbing seconds she did not move. Then her eye-lids flickered and she gave his hand a gentle squeeze.

'Thank God,' he whispered. As he kissed her forehead he thought he felt her cool breath upon his cheek. 'Did you say somethin' darlin'?'

'Smith's men,' she breathed. 'Animals.'

Jed saw red. He had never experienced this kind of overwhelming rage before. It was all consuming. It was pounding in his heart and filling his head like it was about to explode. It carried with it powerful thoughts of revenge and it was unforgiving.

'I'm going to get help for you, Mary-Anne. Be brave. It's all gonna be OK. Just hold on. I'll be as quick as I can.'

As luck would have it, after the incident with the quack doctor, Frank had given Jed the address of a qualified medical man. Doctor Olsen was attending to a young boy who had fallen out of a window but Jed paid no heed to him.

'You got to come with me, Doc. A woman has been raped. It's Mary-Anne.'

'Who?'

'Chrissakes, Doc! Annie Malone! It's serious and if she dies before we get back your life will be on the line.'

'Calm down, young man. I can see you are overwrought and I shall pretend you didn't say that.'

Doctor Olsen was right. Jed was riled and ready to kill Smith in cold blood, even looking forward to it, but dealing with Mary-Anne came first. He knew he needed to be ice-cool and thinking clearly   .

While the Doctor was attending to Mary-Anne at the Parlour the girls began to drift back. They heard the news from Jed with differing reactions. Some were angry, some burst into hysterical tears while others, after cursing soundly set to and started to clear up but all were deeply concerned for Mary-Anne.

After what seemed like an age Doctor Olsen asked for one of the girls to come up and find a nightgown for Mary-Anne after which Jed would be allowed up to see her.

'She is very weak,' cautioned Olsen, 'and traumatised. She can't talk much at the moment. Don't stay long and don't excite her.'

Jed was so pleased to see her awake. To see her blue eyes and her russet-red hair tumbling across the pillow was a joy but he could not ignore the bruises on her face and the cut and swollen lips. Even so, she tried to smile.

'Don't,' he said. 'Please don't. This is all my fault. If'n I'd done something sooner, like you said, this would never have happened. I am so sorry, Mary-Anne. I don't expect forgiveness but I will make it up to you. I promise.'

'Not your fault,' she whispered.

Jed returned to see Mary-Anne the next day and the next and he would have been there again the following day but for yet another killing. Smith's gang had robbed a miner of $3,000 of gold dust. The man had put up a fight but was overcome and thrown into the sea and drowned, leaving a widow and two children. Frank Reid, already incensed by what had happened to Mary-Anne and angered by yet another violent crime in the town, threw caution to the winds and went to see Smith at Jeff's Place. He was so fired up he pushed aside the two henchman, standing guard, and forced his way into the back office. Smith was sitting at his desk smoking a cigar.

'Mr Reid. To what do I owe this unexpected visit.' He waved the two men out of the room.

'You've done enough damage in this town,' raged Frank. 'Two days ago your disgusting pigs violated Annie Malone, and don't tell me you had nothing to do with it. Now you've had another innocent man killed for his gold. There's no way you can undo what happened to Annie but you, sure as hell, can return that man's poke.'

'Well now, I don't think that's any of your business,' said Smith calmly.

'I'm *making* it my business,' said Frank.

And if I don't return the poke?'

'We'll run you out of town so fast your feet won't touch the ground!'

Smith laughed and then deliberately blew a cloud of cigar smoke into Frank's face. 'Are you threatening me? Why, I'm quaking in my boots.'

'Listen up and listen good,' said Frank, leaning on the desk. 'I want that gold returned. I don't care how you do it, but do it! And I'll give you till four o'clock this afternoon - or else!'

'Well, well! An ultimatum!' Smith was still smiling broadly. 'Don't you know that's fighting talk, Frank? But as I've told you before, if you want a fight you can have one.'

'I mean what I say, Smith!'

'Sure you do. Close the door on the way out, will you, Frank?'

Frank went straight round to Annie's Parlour. After enquiring about Mary-Anne, he told Jed what he'd said to Smith.

'You threatened him? And what are you going to do if he don't do what you say?'

'There'll be a showdown. I've got a hundred vigilante's backing me, Jed. Smith's got thirty or forty men at the most. I reckon if it came to a shootout the odds are in our favour. Hell, I'd like to shoot him myself.'

'Stand in line, Frank. After what's happened to Mary-Anne I swear I could kill him with my bare hands.'

'Maybe you could, but this is *my* business. I've started it and I'm going to finish it.'

'But supposin' he *does* return the gold. What then? You're back where you started. Maybe even worse off 'cos who knows what he'll do to get it back again. Look what happened to the Parson! '

'He won't. I know that! But it gives me, us, an excuse to get rid of him. I've called a meeting of the committee officers this afternoon to work out exactly what we'll do.'

'I'll come with you.'

'No. There's nothing I'd like more than to have you join us, Jed, but you've got to stay here. Mary-Anne needs you more than I do right now.'

'You're not holdin' the meetin' at your house again, are you?'

'No. It'll be at that disused warehouse just outside town. Nobody goes there anymore because it's pretty near derelict but I let Smith know this time.'

'Are you crazy? What did you do that fer?'

'To give him the chance to bring the gold back without losing face. I told him I'd wait outside. Nobody need know. But if he wasn't there by four…"

'You're taking one hell of a risk, Frank. Let me come with you as another gun.'

'Thanks, Jed, but no. I told him I'd be on my own and I will be.'

'But supposing *he* isn't.'

That's a chance I've got to take. I've got the committee to back me up if needed.'

'That might be too late. I'm coming with you.'

'No you ain't! I know you've got score to settle with him but, hell, so have I.'

Mary-Anne's health was improving daily and Jed was greatly relieved to see her progressing so well. Nelly was getting on with the business of getting Annie's Parlour up and running again and he called in most afternoons. But that afternoon Jed could not concentrate on small talk and found himself thinking about Frank and his foolhardy ultimatum - and what he might do. He watched the delicate hands on Mary-Anne's mantle clock getting ever closer to the time of the vigilante's meeting. Suddenly, he stood up.

'I'm sorry, Mary-Anne. I've got to leave you for a while. It's important.'

He had managed without a horse since arriving in Skagway and had never needed one - until now. He knew it was possible to get up to that old warehouse on foot but it would take far too long. He eyed the line of horses on the hitching rail out side Annie's Place. Stealing a horse was akin to murder and was a hanging offence but he had to have one, had to have one now. He scanned the sidewalk until he saw a small boy kicking a stone.

'Hey! Sonny. Over here.' The boy looked wary and held back. 'It's OK. I need you to do me a favour.'

Three minute's negotiation, more than Jed intended, and he was on a horse and heading east towards the vigilante's secret meeting place. He had promised to pay the boy five dollars to guard that space while he was away and if the owner returned, to say Jed Hansen had borrowed it and would be bringing it back. But the boy was a sharp as a nail and had demanded half up front as well as a signature.

Luckily, Jed was the first to arrive at the warehouse and had time to conceal the horse. Then he hid behind a rocky outcrop, which not only afforded some shelter but a perfect view of the warehouse below. And not before time. Within minutes the first of the vigilantes arrived, quickly followed by the others. Jed counted ten in all. They tied their horses to a rail and waited. Nobody spoke and Jed could almost feel the tension from his hiding place.

Frank was the last to arrive with a key to the door. Before letting them in Jed heard him say; 'You haven't told anyone where we're meeting, have you?' They all shook their heads. 'Good. While the meeting is on, I intend to stand guard. You carry on and somebody can relieve me later. OK?'

The men went inside. Frank paced up and down for a bit, checking his watch and then his gun, slipping it in and out of its holster. Jed felt uneasy. Frank was no match for a ruthless killer like Smith.

Jed had been watching for twenty minutes before he heard the sound of a horse approaching. He released the safety catch on his gun as he saw Frank tuck his jacket behind his revolver.

Then Smith rode into view. Jed tensed, listening for the sound of other horses but there were none. Unbelievably, it looked as though he had come alone. He got off his horse some twenty yards from where Frank was standing, his face like stone, and Jed's eyes were immediately drawn to the double-barrelled rifle Smith was carrying. He held it low, casual-like, his forefinger resting over the trigger.

'That's far enough,' called out Frank. 'Have you got the gold?'

'No. I ain't! And you know I ain't. I don't know what you're up to, Reid, but you keep sticking you long busybody nose into my business and you sure are riling me. I thought you'd learned by now that I don't play games.' He took a step forward.

'Hold it, Smith. Don't come any closer or...' Frank's hand hovered over his holster.

What happened next was over in a split second. Smith, seeing Frank go for his gun, squeezed the trigger on his rifle. Frank jack-knifed to the ground, bleeding profusely, but as he fell two other shots were simultaneously fired. One came from Frank's gun and the other from Jed's. Frank's bullet winged its way harmlessly into the air but Jed's was deadly accurate. He watched with grim satisfaction as the expression on Smith's face turned into horrified disbelief. He remained upright for a second or two then, as the blood gushed out of his chest, his legs buckled beneath him and Jefferson Smith, the scourge of Skagway, collapsed face down into the dirt.

Jed ran straight over to Frank and was relieved beyond measure to find him alive, though very badly hurt. The sound of gunfire brought the vigilantes running from the warehouse and Jed told them how Smith had fired on Frank without any warning. He also told them how Frank, though badly wounded, had returned his fire. 'Shot that devil clean through the heart,' he lied. 'This man is a hero.'

THE FINAL CHAPTER

Skagway, Alaska, July 1898

Frank was mortally wounded and only survived his killer by twelve days. Jed was devastated by the loss of his courageous friend and made sure that everybody in town knew what a great man he was. When news got out about Frank's death the vigilantes, angry and hell-bent on revenge went into town and shot seven of Smith's men in cold blood. Then they rounded up as many as they could find for a mass lynching. Had it not been for the timely arrival of a United States Infantry Unit, which imposed military law, the lynchings would have surely gone ahead. But with the army in control, law and order was soon restored and Skagway, the last outpost of the wild and lawless West, was conquered.

Annie's Parlour was back in business and looked as good as new, if not better, but Mary-Anne, though fully recovered from her ordeal, no longer had the heart nor the strength to carry on and sold out to Eleanor Weiss, better known as Nelly. Jed, his mission now complete also had no reason to stay in Skagway so he and Mary-Anne moved south. They married and set up home in Idaho where they bought a farm, raised shorthorn cattle and lived out the rest of their lives in peace.

THE END

Historical Notes:

Two of the characters in this book are based on real people -Jefferson Randolph Smith and Frank Reid. Jeff Smith (also known as Soapy Smith) was a skilled swindler and a ruthless criminal - probably the last of West's truly bad men – who brought terror and violence to Skagway. Frank Reid was a civil engineer and surveyor who set up the vigilante Committee of 101 in an attempt to bring about law and order. Harriet (Ma) Pullen also lived at that time and was famous for her pies.

However, all other characters are fictitious, as are the events that surround them. Some are loosely based on true happenings but any resemblance to real people living or dead is purely co-incidental.